Ginger's Shoes

A Lake Hopatcong Mystery

Steve Lindahl

"A lake carries you into recesses of feeling otherwise impenetrable."

- William Wordsworth

Chapter One

2022

*F*ind *Ginger's shoes.* That's what Nancy Walsh would tell her daughter. If Susie followed the clues, she would discover the confusing circumstances and understand why Nancy had waited so long. Yet Nancy knew her own body well enough to realize she had to speak up soon. This would be her final puzzle.

* * *

For her entire life, Susie's mom loved puzzles, mysteries, and challenges. When Susie was growing up, there was often a jigsaw puzzle on the dining room table alongside a copy of the Sunday New York Times, opened to the crossword.

Nancy referred to herself as a problem solver, but she also enjoyed creating challenges for other people, especially her daughter. She enjoyed hiding Easter eggs so much, she made a hunt part of their Christmas tradition by hiding Susie's smaller presents. Susie remembered her mother's favorite saying. "When you work to achieve something, it becomes more valuable."

When Susie was a child she had to work harder to get the simplest things but now understood why. Nancy's love of challenges was something that made her an exceptional mother. When Susie experienced any of the issues common to young girls Nancy would make a game out of handling them. She wasn't a helicopter mother. She would help her daughter find her own solutions.

Many things went unsaid between them but not the normal omissions other mothers and daughters might regret. They had expressed their love for each other every day since Nancy became sick. They had spent as much time together as possible, often rehashing old memories.

COPD was unexpected because Nancy was a non-smoker and they lived in Morris County, New Jersey, an area where there wasn't a lot of air pollution. Whatever the cause was, she had to deal with it, which meant huffing and puffing in the beginning, then carrying an oxygen tank with her wherever she went, and finally, having to move to a nursing home where Susie continued to visit her mother every day.

* * *

Nancy's chin trembled. "There are things I've never told you." She coughed.

"What are those *things*?"

Nancy coughed again. "Things that are too important to just tell you."

"Is this another one of your puzzles, Mom?"

"Yes. But the most important one I'll ever give you because it's about me and you and…well, you'll see. I'll give you hints if you get stuck and if you can't find the answer I'll tell you everything." She was breathing fast.

"Relax, Mom. You're getting stressed. It can wait."

"I suppose it can but let me say one thing." Nancy paused as her breathing slowed, then she spoke in a soft voice. "Find Ginger's shoes."

"What was that?"

Nancy took Susie's hand. She chuckled softly then repeated, "Find Ginger's shoes." She coughed again. "I didn't keep them in our house where you might discover them but you will know where to look first. I'm certain of that."

Susie shook her head. "I don't want to waste time looking for some old shoes. I want to be here with you."

"The shoes are important. When you find them, you will treasure them. That's all I'm going to say. I'm tired. I'll explain more tomorrow."

Nancy's voice trailed off to a whisper so soft Susie had trouble understanding.

"What?"

"Tomorrow."

"All right. You know I love you, right?" Susie smiled and kissed her cheek.

Nancy nodded and closed her eyes.

* * *

Susie's phone rang at two AM and she realized her greatest fear. It was the nursing home. "Your mother had a heart attack. Her eyes are open and she's breathing but given her condition, we don't believe she'll survive the night. You better come in as quickly as you can."

It had been a long day and Susie had been in deep sleep but those words had her heart racing and her adrenaline pumping. She tore off her nightgown, grabbed the jeans and t-shirt she'd worn the day before, dressed quickly, and headed out of her apartment. She didn't even brush her hair. While she drove Susie prayed her mom would stay alive long enough to speak to her one more time.

There was almost no traffic on the dark roads. She could drive fast. But at the nurse's station, they informed Susie her mother had died ten minutes earlier.

When she stepped into the room a different nurse, a man, was by Nancy's bed, disconnecting her oxygen and the equipment used to monitor her. He looked up from his task and stared at Susie's eyes.

Susie's body tensed. Her eyes were crystal-blue and wet since she'd been crying but that was no reason for him to stare. She kept her focus on her mother and shook her head slowly, her muscles quivering.

The nurse brought his hand to his chest. "I…I'm sorry." He stuttered. "I was startled. That was all. I didn't mean to…"

"Can I be alone with her?" Susie interrupted without looking at him.

"Of course," he told her as he scurried out of the room.

That thoughtless man had reminded her of the ways she and her brown-eyed mother looked different. She had just lost the best friend she'd ever had and because of him their differences were cascading through her mind like flood waters. She and her mother were about the same height but Susie's face was rounder with a wider chin. Her hair was blond while Nancy's was mid-brown. Their eyes were the biggest difference but Susie had always attributed the blue color to her parents both having recessive genes.

Susie bent over her mother and kissed her forehead. She climbed onto the bed, lay beside the mother she loved so deeply, and buried her face in Nancy's neck. Susie had hugged her mom after some of the most hurtful days of her life. There was the time a teacher had accused her of cheating and the time a boy she liked had stood her up, and then there was the day her father died, the only other pain that had come close to this. Now here she was, crying again on her mother's shoulder and this time the woman who had helped her through those dark times was gone forever.

Tears were flowing down Susie's cheeks. Her nose was running. She had an ache in her chest and the world seemed to spin. Where could she turn? Who would help her get through this grief and pain?

She kept her arms around her mother until a different nurse came into the room and tapped her on the shoulder.

"I'm sorry," the woman whispered. "I have to ask you to leave. We have somewhere else where you can lie down if you're too weak to drive but we need to move your mother to a place where we can take care of her properly."

Susie didn't move, although she acknowledged the woman with a sigh.

"Please," the nurse told her. "I can help you walk or I can get you a wheelchair."

* * *

It had been a sad journey into the late stages of Nancy's disease although Susie had felt closer to her mother. That was nice, but those few good feelings hadn't stopped the inevitable.

A few days before Nancy moved to the nursing home, the mother and daughter had a wonderful heart-to-heart.

"I had an amazing life. I wouldn't change a thing." She took her daughter's hand and held it as tightly as she could.

"You wouldn't?" Susie pulled her hair into a ponytail and held it there with an elastic band. "But what about Dad? Wouldn't you have stopped the accident?"

"What I mean is I wouldn't change anything I had control over."

Susie understood what Nancy was saying. She was talking about her career as an actress and how she'd given it up to raise Susie. Nancy had performed in a few off-broadway shows, including playing Eva in *Last Summer at Bluefish Cove* but that was a long time ago.

Her mom had been a sweet-natured optimist. She'd always said she loved her life, especially their house at the lake and watching over Susie when they lived there. She was not the type of person to have any regrets.

Susie grasped her mother's arm. "We had some wonderful times on that beautiful island, didn't we?"

Nancy nodded.

"It was a shame we had to give it up," Susie told her. "That was another thing beyond your control, right?"

Nancy shrugged, and Susie smiled.

They reminisced until Nancy was too tired to keep her eyes open.

Chapter Two

Thirteen Years Earlier

Susie Walsh and Kyle Olsen were in the sixth grade at Briggs Elementary, Miss Esposito's class. They had been in the same classes since the first grade and were best friends.

Susie invited Kyle to her eleventh birthday party, telling him he was first on her list. He was excited because he had been to her lake house many times over the past few summers and had enjoyed his time there. During his last visit, she took him on a hike to the center of the island even though it was an overcast day with drizzle. It was fun walking through wet grass and climbing over fallen trees. When they returned to the house, they played their Narnia game in her room.

His favorite part was when they hid in her wardrobe. He loved closing the door and standing in the dark beside her, the clothes she kept on hangers wrapping around them like small blankets. They always tried to be quiet as they pretended they were being carried off to the imaginary world of Aslan, the great lion. But after a while one of them would laugh and when that happened they had to step out into the light of her bedroom.

Susie's parents planned the party for Saturday, September sixteenth, because her actual birthday, the fifteenth, fell on a school day. The day was warm and sunny with just a few slow-moving, white clouds in the sky. It was more like midsummer than fall.

Kyle's mom and grandfather were going with him to the party. "I'll help watch the kids," she told Kyle. "With so many kids in and out of the water, Susie's mom will need a few extra adults keeping their eyes open. As for Grandpa, he wants to go just because he loves talking with Susie's parents. He says he plans to help. We'll see if that happens."

They parked their car near Main Lake Market where Susie's father picked them up. There was no bridge or ferry connecting Halsey Island to the mainland so he had to give boat rides to all the party guests. The ride in an aluminum rowboat with a small outboard motor disappointed Kyle. He had hoped to ride in Mr. Walsh's Chris-Craft, one of the coolest boats Kyle had ever seen, but Susie's dad told him it was stored for the season.

When they reached the Walsh's dock, Kyle noticed some kids were already swimming. Susie was in the lake but came out to greet him. The wet locks of her blond hair fell over her small shoulders in rope-like bunches. Her two-piece bathing suit was pink with pictures of yellow bananas on both the top and the bottom. Susie's crystal-blue eyes made her wide smile seem as bright as the sun over the lake.

Kyle looked around the dock, noticing the others at the party were all girls. He didn't think girls were silly and a waste of time like some of his friends did. There were plenty of things girls could do just as well as boys, like board games and stuff, and Susie was the best. She could do anything any boy could do. But still—he was the *only* boy there. He stuck out like a feather on a fish.

Kyle was holding Susie's gift, so he tried to hand it to her. She laughed at him. "Not now, silly. I'm all wet." She was right. Her hair was dripping. "You need to take it up to the house. There's a table on the porch with drinks and snacks. Put it there."

Kyle headed off the dock toward her house. He knew Susie would like his gift. She had a Nintendo and had hinted she wanted *The Legend of Zelda: Twilight Princess.* Kyle hoped he was the only one who got it for her, but his mom said it was exchangeable if there was a problem.

"Kyle," Susie yelled. "Put on your suit when you're up there."

He looked at his mom who lifted a bag she was holding. Kyle turned to get it from her before heading up the hill. Once he reached the house, he found the table on their porch. He put down the gift and grabbed a handful of potato chips and pretzels. The cake was on the table but they hadn't cut it yet so he guessed it was for later.

Kyle stuffed the chips and two pretzels into his mouth, then headed for the door to the inside of the house. He remembered the upstairs bathroom, a place where he could change. Kyle went through the front door and into the living room.

This was the largest room in the house, wrapping toward his right, then to the back where there was a round dining table. A piano was off to the side. Susie had told Kyle she was taking lessons.

On the left side of the living room, there were stairs leading to the second floor. He walked past them and peeked into the kitchen. The scent of the freshly baked cake was still in the room. It made him hungry even though he'd just eaten snacks. Kyle was tempted to run back to the front porch and grab a finger full of icing but he just walked to the living room.

The dark brown walls, along with the deer head and several duck decoys displayed on high shelves made the place feel like one of the lodges at Minisink, a camp Kyle had attended for a couple of weeks in July.

He climbed the stairs to the upstairs hall. The bathroom he was looking for was on the opposite side of the hall but he glanced to his left into Susie's bedroom and walked in that direction. He remembered the Narnia game they had played there. That was fun.

She had a plain bed with no fancy bedposts as you might expect in a girl's room. Next to the bed was a neat, blue, inflatable chair, which wasn't there the last time he'd been in the room. He could see Susie taking it down to the lake and tossing it in the water to use as a raft. How much fun would that be?

The bed was in the corner of the room and the wall next to it was covered with pictures of Nick Carter and the Backstreet Boys. They weren't there the last time Kyle had visited Susie. There was the white bureau and the wardrobe, the one they had hidden inside when they pretended to be on their way to Narnia.

He turned around, went to her desk, and sat in the chair. Susie's reading and arithmetic books were stacked there. Since they were both in Briggs Elementary, Kyle had the same books. Next to those she had a pad of paper with a list of some books Miss Esposito had recommended for summer reading and some algebra problems Susie had been working out.

That's when he saw his name. Susie had written "Kyle" at the top of the paper and next to his name she'd drawn a heart. He couldn't believe it. Susie liked him. He always knew she liked to pal around with him. After all, he was the only boy she invited to her party. But this was different. She had been sitting up here, trying to do her homework while thinking about him! Kyle felt his stomach flutter. He picked up the pad, looked at it closer, then tried to set it back in the same position. He didn't want Susie to notice he'd been looking through her stuff.

Kyle grabbed the bag with his bathing suit. He headed toward the bathroom to change when he heard music coming from a room down the hall. He wondered who would be in the house while the party was down by the lake.

He tiptoed along the hallway. The music was coming from another bedroom, one on the lakeside of the house. The door was open and Kyle could see Susie's mom watching TV. She was angled away from the door where he was standing. He could see the side of her face as well as what she was watching—an old movie with a couple dancing and singing. This seemed odd to Kyle. Here was Susie's mom, so into what was on TV she hadn't noticed him standing there. His own mom, his grandfather, and three other adults were watching the kids swim, but this was the Walsh's party. Susie's mom should have been with them.

She was leaning toward the TV, focused completely on the couple dancing. They were singing the words "dancing cheek to cheek" over and over. Kyle had never heard that song but he liked it.

The man was dressed in black with a white shirt and tie and the woman was wearing a dress covered with feathers. They moved together like waves on the lake.

Meanwhile, Susie's mom sat there holding a high-heeled shoe, turning it over and over in her hands. Her eyes were wet and Kyle thought she was crying. A substance that looked like silver glitter covered the shoe. Every once in a while it would catch light from the window and flash at him.

Kyle didn't want to disturb her so he went back to the bathroom, put on his bathing suit, and headed down to join Susie and the others in the water. On his way across the lawn, he glanced back at the upstairs bedroom window and wondered why Susie's mom was waiting so long to join her guests.

Chapter Three

Two Years After Susie's Party

Nancy sold both their summer and winter homes after Susie's father, Scott, died in an accident. He had been working behind their island house, taking down an ash tree infested with emerald ash borers. The tree fell wrong and crushed him.

Nancy called 9-1-1, then took Susie to the dock where they could hold each other while they waited. It took hours for a crew to get to the island and clear the branches enough to remove his body. After that horrible day, Nancy decided they needed to move far from Lake Hopatcong. She pulled Susie out of Briggs Elementary even though the school year had started. Susie did not want to move but since she was only thirteen years old, her mom didn't listen to her. They moved to a two-bedroom apartment in Flanders.

"I'll buy the lake house for what it's worth," Kyle's grandpa told them, "plus five percent. That way you'll always be welcome here."

His grandfather's purchase eased Kyle's loss of his friend. When Susie stopped spending summers in the lake house, Kyle's family took it over.

He chose the room that had been Susie's for his bedroom and, since they bought the house furnished, he slept in her bed. Kyle found a few things Susie forgot to take with her, including a stuffed cat, a Barbie Swim 'n Dive doll, and a copy of *The Pink Umbrella,* all things she'd outgrown. The book was young for Kyle and a girls' book, but he read it over and over.

When Kyle was fifteen his grandfather died. Six years later his parents moved to Sweden after his father landed a position at Ericsson in Stockholm. Kyle was a junior at Rutgers. He never visited their new home but saw them every Christmas when they returned to America.

Kyle stayed alone in the island home until he asked Taylor Green to move in with him. Taylor, who was a year younger than Kyle, had attended Fairleigh Dickinson where she'd earned a degree in Accounting, finishing a year early by taking summer classes. They both worked at Wyndham Hotels & Resorts in Parsippany. Kyle was the Human Resource Manager and Taylor was an Accountant.

Kyle rented a boat slip on the mainland and used a boat to get to his home. Each year he would stay there from mid-April until late October then move to a small apartment when the lake started to freeze.

When Taylor saw Kyle's winter apartment, she suggested he give it up. "I'll keep my place. I've still got eight months on the lease and with three bedrooms we'll have more room."

Kyle thought how nice it would be to live closer to work in the winter months. He smiled and nodded. "I like that idea. You'll be living with me half the year and I'll be living with you the other half."

"Not *exactly* half."

Kyle laughed because her comment was so typical of an accountant. She laughed, too, and hugged him.

Living on the island was an odd lifestyle, very private in late autumn and early spring but very public in mid-summer when every size boat from paddleboards to the *Miss Lotta*, a double-decker cruise boat, crowded the lake. In comparison, Taylor's apartment was never private. They could hear people upstairs moving around and they parked in a parking lot they shared with their neighbors.

Two days after Taylor moved into the island home, she asked Kyle if they could switch their bedroom. "The other bed is a queen rather than a full," she pointed out, crinkling her nose and furrowing her brow. "I love you, but I could use a little more room—when we're sleeping." She smiled and winked. "Also, the windows look out at the lake rather than back at the woods and there are actual closets, one for each of us rather than sharing a small wardrobe."

"Not a good idea," he told her, stepping back as he spoke. "That's my parents' room."

"I thought you said they don't stay here when they come to America."

Kyle shook his head. "They don't, since this house is hard to get to. But just in case, we shouldn't change things too much."

Taylor accepted Kyle's argument, probably because she had just moved in and didn't want to challenge him. The truth was his parents stayed at a hotel even on the rare occasions when they came during the warm weather. The real reason he didn't want to change bedrooms was he still liked the idea of being in Susie's bed.

Chapter Four

2022

Susie's mother had said Susie would know where to look for the shoes. Because they weren't at her apartment, there was only one place that qualified, the Halsey Island house.

She didn't know Kyle's phone number but, after a quick internet search, she found he worked for Wyndham Hotels. She could have reached him there but decided it would be better to drop by the island house unannounced. When they were young, he loved the lake as much as she did. He probably still lived there.

Susie hadn't been on Lake Hopatcong in years but found a place where she could rent a ski boat. She dressed in a conservative, one-piece bathing suit with black, gray, and white diagonal stripes, then put on a straw hat and a pair of dark sunglasses, to protect her sensitive eyes.

The marina gave Susie a Supra, at least that's what it said on the side of the boat. She could recognize a ski boat but didn't know one brand from another. Any boat would do. She only wanted transportation for one trip from the marina to her old house. When she was out on the open lake, she found the boat was powerful, but as long as she didn't push it too hard it seemed easy enough to control.

She was expecting the house to be quiet. Her intention was to tie at the dock, walk the hill to the house, then knock on the door. Hopefully, Kyle would be home. But when she circled the island she discovered there was a lot of activity on the property.

There must have been fifteen people on the dock and in the swim area. There were even more by the house. Susie decided to find out what was going on. She pulled up where there were dockside boat bumpers and held on until someone came to help her. A man took her bow rope while she tied the one at the stern.

"What's going on?" she asked the guy who had helped her.

He stood up straight, pulled his stomach in, and smiled. "We're having a party. We all work together. Are you a friend of Kyle's?"

"You could say that. I was out on the lake and decided I would stop by to see if he was home."

At that moment, an attractive young woman came out on the dock and walked toward her. She was a little shorter than Susie with skin a bit darker than hers and with long brown hair. Her figure reminded Susie of the Barbie doll she'd left in the house when she was eleven. She wondered if that doll was still hanging around somewhere.

The woman had on a blue bikini with a bandeau top. Compared to the woman's suit, Susie was wearing a burka. This young lady had a smooth, oval face which Susie immediately compared to her round one. She was envious until she saw the woman's eyes were brown, not as intense as Susie's blue ones. Also, her thin nose was not as cute as Susie's. It wasn't normal for her to compare herself with every woman she met but this lady had greeted her in a way that showed she was connected to Kyle. The search for the shoes might take a while and the last thing Susie needed was someone who would not like her spending time with him.

"May I help you?" the young lady asked.

"I hope so. I'm looking for Kyle Olsen. We were friends when we were young."

The woman cocked her head to her left and then asked in a soothing voice, "And you are?"

"Susie Walsh. We were thirteen years old when I last saw Kyle."

"Oh yes. He's mentioned you countless times."

Susie's head jerked back. She hadn't expected that.

The woman moved closer. "Nice boat," she said, leaning forward to look it over.

"It's a rental. I haven't been on Lake Hopatcong in years." Susie pulled her shoulders back and looked up. "I was feeling nostalgic, and the weather was nice so I called around until I found a place that rents. I know my way around boats. I have a friend I ski with." The woman raised her eyebrows so Susie added, "On Greenwood Lake."

"I'm Taylor." She held out her hand. "Let me help you out." When Susie was on the dock Taylor looked her up and down. "It's funny. I always pictured you with brown hair."

"Nope. Always blond. My hair was even lighter when Kyle knew me."

Taylor pulled on the black crochet cover-up she'd bought for the party, then led Susie up the hill to where Kyle was talking to Charles, Taylor's supervisor. She had asked Kyle to watch over Charles. Charles was nice and a perfect boss but awkward in social situations. Taylor wanted this party to leave him with a fond memory of his time at their home. Kyle could talk to anyone, which is why he was a perfect HR Manager.

Taylor had been about to join the swimmers in the lake when Susie arrived. Fortunately, she noticed the boat just before she dove in. Taylor would have hated to be dripping wet when she met the woman who seemed to haunt Kyle. Susie was no longer thirteen, was very attractive, and seemed to be a woman Taylor would like to impress.

They went up the steps onto the porch where Taylor heard Charles say, "I think you got that wrong, Kyle. Last year Rutgers beat Clemson in the first round and lost to Houston in the second. Houston made it to the Final Four then lost to Baylor, who went on to win the tournament." Taylor tried to suppress a smile. She knew Kyle had little interest in sports but here he was showing enough knowledge about the teams in the New York/New Jersey area to get conversations going with people who cared about that stuff.

The men stopped talking when the women arrived. Kyle and Charles looked at Susie with expressions showing they didn't know who she was.

"This is Susie," Taylor told Kyle. "She came to see you." He looked more confused than ever.

Susie took off her sunglasses to reveal the most intense blue eyes Taylor had ever seen. Her irises were like crystal jewels. Taylor felt a flutter in her belly.

"Susie Walsh?" Kyle stared, his mouth open.

She nodded, then put her sunglasses back on.

Kyle jumped and hugged Susie. The way he grabbed her released a tsunami of emotions that had grown inside Taylor every time he had mentioned Susie's name. Taylor felt cold but also angry, jealous, and interested at the same time. She knew Susie was important to Kyle. He had told her countless stories, repeating some of them to where Taylor knew every word he was about to say. She hated how he felt about her but understood why. He had spoken about her so many times she felt as if she knew Susie. Now Taylor wanted her chance to be close enough to Susie to look through her eyes and see her soul.

When Kyle finally released his hold on Susie (or vice versa, Taylor couldn't tell for sure), they took seats on the wicker furniture, she on the settee and he on the rocker. They started asking the kinds of questions anyone would ask someone they hadn't seen in twelve years.

Susie was a receptionist at the dentist's office where her mom had been a hygienist. It was a perfect job since her work schedule allowed her plenty of time to be involved with plays at the Chester Theatre, sometimes on stage and sometimes working behind the set. She'd picked up her interest in theater from her mother who'd had a modest professional career before Susie was born. Kyle asked what roles she had performed.

Taylor turned toward Charles who was leaning on the porch railing, looking half asleep as he stared down at the people mingling on the dock. "Well, Charles," she said. "We should leave these two to reminisce. Have you ever played bocce?"

He shook his head.

"We've got a set in the back. I'll show you how. It's a combination of bowling and pool. I'm not very good. I can almost guarantee you'll beat me, but it will still be fun."

She took his arm in hers and led him through the house to the backyard. As they left the porch, she waved to Kyle but neither he nor Susie noticed. They were focused on each other. Taylor felt her stomach harden. She wasn't sure if she wanted more attention from Kyle or his long-lost friend.

Chapter Five

Kyle and Susie had a strong friendship when they were kids but nothing beyond that. They had been too young for romance. Once, during the summer between their fourth and fifth grades, they went into Susie's boathouse and did the *I'll show you mine if you show me yours thing* kids do. But that was just curiosity. Their hormones weren't controlling their minds back then. Sometimes Susie longed to go back to that innocent time. Her own search for love had led to many short-term relationships. Those had been mostly lonely and tiring, although there was still hope for her and Danny.

Susie had flirted with Danny for weeks before he asked her out. He was a rep from the company that made crowns for the dentist's office where she worked. Danny told Susie he loved theater. He had never been on stage but said he enjoyed attending shows. He had majored in History at Rutgers where his favorite course had been Theater History.

They had dinner at the Blue Morel Restaurant in Morristown after which they headed over to The New Jersey Shakespeare Festival to see a production of *Pride and Prejudice*. To Susie, this was a perfect first date.

Most of Susie's time with Kyle had been at their school or his house. He lived close to Briggs Elementary and his mom allowed Susie to stay at their place when Susie's mom was busy. Susie's family paid the Olsens back by inviting Kyle to their house on Halsey Island a few times each summer.

Kyle and Susie talked for ten minutes about his job at Wyndham and how he received discounts on hotel rooms across the country. He had traveled a lot. Most of his journeys were on his own but he had taken a couple of trips recently with Taylor: one to Aruba and one to Niagara Falls.

"Niagara Falls?" she asked, raising her eyebrows. "Wasn't that once called the honeymoon capital of the world?"

He laughed. "No. Not a honeymoon, if that's what you're thinking. Taylor and I have been together for over a year and we're starting to consider marriage but we haven't made any definite plans."

It was good they weren't married. Susie pressed two fingers to her lips to stop the smile she felt coming.

When he asked about her life Susie talked about how much she loved the theater at Chester and how he should see some shows. When the small talk petered out, she decided it was time to bring up the real reason she was there.

Susie tightened her fists and leaned toward Kyle. "Can I ask you something, Kyle? You see, my mom died recently."

She saw him flinch. He had known her mother well when he was a child. "On the last day she was alive, she asked me to find Ginger's shoes. I have no idea what she meant, but I thought of the story you told me, of how you saw her upstairs during my sixth-grade party, holding a shoe, and watching an old movie."

"I'm sorry to hear she passed. She was a wonderful woman."

"Thank you. But do you know anything about those old shoes? It was her deathbed wish for me to find them."

"I know about one of them. It was a silver high-heeled shoe that sparkled with glitter. Your family left it here after we bought your house. My grandfather put it somewhere but I don't know where. He showed it to me before he stored it. Ginger Rogers' name is on the shoe and I think it might be an authentic autograph. When my great-grandfather was a boy he used to do odd jobs for Joe Cook. Cook was a Vaudeville performer who owned a house on the lake. He threw wild parties like the ones in *The Great Gatsby*. A lot of celebrities partied there including Ginger Rogers and even Babe Ruth and Groucho Marx. Their names are on a piano Cook used to own, which is now at the Hopatcong Museum. It's possible Joe Cook, or even Ginger herself, gave my great-grandfather that shoe and she signed it."

"But you said my mom had a shoe at my party. We still owned the house back then. Why would she have had something that was your great-grandfather's?"

"He was gone way before the time you turned eleven. Your mother probably got it from my grandfather. Our families were always close. Maybe he gave it to her? Could she have been a Ginger Rogers fan?"

"I suppose so."

"I do have to get back to my guests so I can't look for it today. Can you come back tomorrow?"

Kyle asked Susie to stay for the party but she declined saying she'd be out of place at his office party and he didn't insist. Instead, he walked her to her boat. As soon as he saw the Supra, he commented on how sleek it looked.

"Taylor said the same thing, but it's just a rental."

"You shouldn't have to pay for a boat to visit me."

She laughed. "You live on an island. Is there another way I don't know about?"

"Tomorrow I'll pick you up at Main Lake Market. Call me when you get there."

As Susie climbed into the boat, Kyle remembered her father arriving in his little aluminum boat to pick up the children for her birthday party. He hadn't driven the Chris-Craft because they had stored it for the winter. Kyle's grandfather had bought it along with the house and kept everything in great condition. Tomorrow, Kyle would be in that beautiful boat. He was certain it would trigger some memories for her.

Susie pulled her phone out of the purse she'd left under the steering wheel and added his number to her contacts. When she was done, Kyle untied the boat and watched her ride away.

Chapter Six

The next day was Sunday and, as was their tradition, Taylor and Kyle were enjoying breakfast together—coffee and Taylor's blueberry pancakes. They were going over the events of the previous day. Taylor had been quite proud of the way she'd prepared the house and how all the children of their co-workers seemed to enjoy themselves in the water.

"One thing, though." Taylor frowned. "It was strange how your old girlfriend, Susie, showed up. You hadn't invited her, had you?"

Kyle noticed her frown. "Old girlfriend? We were thirteen when I last saw her, too young for anything like that."

"Yeah. Whatever."

"Not a girlfriend, but just so you know, she *is* coming back today."

"Is she? Why?"

"She's looking for a pair of shoes."

"Really?"

"They belonged either to her mother or my grandfather. I'm not sure which. Anyway, her mother talked about them on her deathbed."

"Her mother died?"

"Just recently. That's why Susie is looking for the shoes."

Taylor rubbed the back of her neck. "I'm sorry. I didn't know."

"No need. You were nice to her, right?"

Taylor wrinkled her nose. "Of course." She paused. "I still don't understand about the shoes."

"They are collectibles with Ginger Roger's name on them. Perhaps they were ones she wore in a film. Susie's mother told her to find them. It was the last thing she said." Taylor looked down at her coffee as Kyle continued to speak. "I saw her mother holding one of them at that party when Susie turned eleven. That was a long time ago. Years later, my grandfather showed me the same shoe. I can't imagine him throwing it out. We knew Susie's family. They were friends. We didn't feel as if we were moving into a stranger's house. We kept their furniture, their boats, their garden tools, and lots of boxes we've never gone through. Maybe she's right."

Taylor bit her lower lip, still looking down. Kyle knew that habit of hers. It meant she was hiding something. He hoped she hadn't been lying when she said she'd been nice to Susie.

Susie called the next morning at eleven. Sunday was the day Taylor shopped for groceries but this time she was home. Kyle thought her staying on the island had to do with Susie coming by again.

Taylor stepped toward him as he put his phone back in his pocket. "I want to go with you to pick her up."

"That's unnecessary."

"I know, but it's what I want to do."

He felt his stomach turn. "You are okay with this, right?"

"And what would you do if I wasn't?"

That was not the answer he was hoping for. "I would try to explain why I have to help her."

"That's what I thought." She shook her head. "You're a sweet person, Kyle. That's one reason I love you." She took his hand in hers. "I think I may be a little jealous. I've heard her name over and over and now I've seen her. She's stunning, you know, especially those eyes of hers. But you should know me well enough to know I won't stop you from helping her. I mean, her mother's deathbed wish? The fact is, I want to help her, too. You won't deny me that. Will you?"

Chapter Seven

Before she was with Kyle, Taylor cooked on Sundays. She lived alone and most of the simple recipes she used provided enough for a family of four. Taylor would decide what she was in the mood to eat that week and prepare enough to last her until the next Sunday. That way all she had to do each evening was warm a plate of food, eat it, and clean up. The following week she would cook something different.

Her on-again-off-again romantic life was similar. She had relationships that would keep her going for a while, then she would break them off. She would get by alone until she felt lonely. At that point, Taylor would find someone new to be with.

For at least two years after her first experience with sex, she'd been with men only. She had liked most of them but some were a little rough. She was nineteen when she was first intimate with a woman. That experience with Camilla differed from what she'd known with men. It was softer and gentler.

Camilla and Taylor were both in an *Intro to Statistics* class even though Camilla was in her third year. Neither of them liked the teacher and enjoyed making up jokes about him which they shared over drinks and burgers at Prospect Tavern in Madison. Camilla would enjoy a glass of wine while Taylor, being underage, sipped on a Coke. After a couple of visits to the tavern, Taylor complained about wanting something stronger than cola. When the next Statistics class was over, they ended up drinking in Camilla's dorm room.

Camilla poured each of them a glass of Sauvignon Blanc, then put a CD in her computer drive. It was *Songbird* by Eva Cassidy. Camilla had a couple of quality speakers hooked to her laptop so the sound was decent.

Taylor smiled while Camilla sat on her bed and gestured for Taylor to sit on the floor in front of her. "Your hair looks inviting. I'd like to brush it. Is that all right?"

Taylor nodded and sat down, leaning back against the bed while Camilla wrapped her legs around her. Camilla didn't use a brush. Instead, she ran her fingers through Taylor's hair softly which, combined with the wine, made Taylor feel warm.

Only two men had ever concentrated on Taylor's hair before sex and they had both pulled rather than stroked. Perhaps they were trying to dominate or maybe they were simply awkward. Either way, she liked what Camilla was doing much more.

It didn't take long before Camilla reached down, pulled up Taylor's shirt, and ran her fingers under the band of Taylor's bra. The caresses that followed led to Camilla leaning over and kissing Taylor. It was a weird kiss since Camilla's head was upside down, like in that scene from the old Spiderman movie with Kirsten Dunst but it had an emotional punch Taylor will never forget.

That was their first time together and there were a few more but eventually Camilla grew tired and moved on. Taylor had more affairs with men than with women after Camilla but nothing stuck with either gender until she met Kyle.

When Kyle asked Taylor out, her life changed. Their first date was for dinner and a film. They ate at Alice's on the shore of Lake Hopatcong then drove to Succasunna where they saw a Jennifer Lopez film. The movie was silly but cute. She enjoyed it.

Their next date was dinner at Ruth's Chris Steak House where the food and atmosphere were wonderful. But they worried someone might see them. The two of them dating wasn't against company rules since Kyle wasn't her manager, but the restaurant is in the Parsippany Hilton. Two employees of Wyndham patronizing a Hilton would be frowned on especially since Kyle was in management. Taylor suggested the restaurant and was pleased Kyle had agreed. There was something exciting about breaking their company's unwritten rule.

He didn't ask if Taylor wanted him to get a room after they were done with their meal, which was a disappointment. She would have said no, but she wanted him to ask. Instead, they stayed at their table for more than an hour. They sipped coffee and talked. Her conversations with other people she'd dated were so boring she had trouble remembering one from another. The men always talked about the weather, traveling, and odd things like slow internet connections or getting stuck in traffic. The women talked about clothes, skincare, hairstyles, and reality TV.

Kyle was different. He spoke about things he did away from work. Kyle had bought a beat-up old Thistle sailboat he'd spent months restoring and now enjoyed sailing on Lake Hopatcong. He had raced it a few times but had always ended up in the middle of the pack. He didn't mind not winning. It was working with the wood and fiberglass he enjoyed and, most of all, he loved looking at the finished product after he'd made it shine.

At the restaurant, Kyle asked her what she loved. "Not who—what," he said. "Loving other people is important, but it's also important to have something you dream about, something that is yours alone."

Taylor smoothed her dress and then glanced into his eyes. She felt an unusual connection to him, which is why she explained the reason she worked in accounting. "When I was a child, I had all the normal little girl dreams." She winked at him then reached across the table and took his hand. "I wanted to be an actress or a model or a dancer. I probably shouldn't say this because it will make me sound full of myself, but people around me told me I had the looks for any of those dream jobs."

He chuckled, then said, "You *are* beautiful."

"Please, I'm not fishing."

"I didn't think you were."

Taylor smiled. "Anyway, I took dance but found I didn't like it half as much as I liked arithmetic. I know that sounds weird, but I love the feeling I get when my answers check out."

"So you discovered you wanted to crunch numbers?"

He didn't laugh, and she appreciated it. She nodded.

"That's wonderful. You know yourself well and you got the job you wanted. But you should keep dreaming."

Taylor released Kyle's hand and sat up straight. She ran her fingers through her hair and flipped both sides over her shoulders. She widened her eyes, smiled, and said, "I have other dreams."

Kyle must have understood her meaning because he asked her to dinner again while they were still in the restaurant. This time he offered to cook for her at his island home on Lake Hopatcong. She reached her foot out to touch his leg under the table and said, "I'd love that."

When they left the restaurant, he took her back to her apartment and kissed her at her front door. She didn't suggest he come inside but she suspected they would finally get together at his house.

A week later Kyle picked Taylor up and drove her to Bridge Marina on Lake Hopatcong, the place where he kept his Chris-Craft. It was still May, but the evening was warm. They drove the boat away from the Marina and went under a bridge. When they had passed a buoy marking a slow speed zone, he gunned the engine, and they took off. Taylor had carefully combed her hair and now it was blowing all over the place. Her hair was a mess, but she loved the ride. She had little experience in boats so zipping through the water was exciting. There were a few other boats making waves on the lake but the Chris-Craft was solid and the ride smooth. Still, Taylor was breathing hard when they reached Kyle's home. They tied up toward the front of his dock and walked to the house.

Kyle's home was at the top of a hill. It was a white, two-story Victorian with three dormers on the second floor and a two-sided, wrap-around porch on the first. Taylor felt at ease with the world. She stopped for a moment and turned to look at the wide expanse of the lake below them, then back at the porch. She pictured herself sitting there, rocking on a porch chair, watching the boats, feeling a soft breeze. In a place like this, Taylor could be happy.

Kyle grilled salmon, boiled red potatoes, and stir-fried some mixed vegetables. It wasn't an exotic meal but Taylor enjoyed it. They ate on his front porch. After they were done with their meal and most of a bottle of White Zinfandel, he offered a canoe ride. When she told him she didn't know how to paddle he said, "That's fine. It's even better. Instead of putting you in the front, I'll put you in a canoe seat on the floor of the boat where you can stretch your legs and look back at me. That way we can talk while I paddle."

They did a figure-eight around the two islands: Halsey and Raccoon. They passed two islets beside Raccoon Island then went around a point and through a channel where there was a small, two-car ferry. On the way back, they passed Main Lake Market on the mainland. It was a beautiful, peaceful ride. Even though Kyle had said he would talk as he paddled, he spoke little. Taylor was glad because she was busy enjoying the fresh smell of the water, the light breeze, and the sounds of frogs and insects when they were close to land. The setting sun cast a soft glow over the shoreline. Taylor didn't think there could be a prettier place in the world.

When they finished their ride Kyle helped Taylor out and pulled the canoe up on the dock. They went back to the porch and opened another bottle of wine, a cabernet this time. They each had two more glasses after which he took her hand and led her to his bedroom.

Sex with Kyle was great for Taylor that first time and every time since. In the beginning, it was exciting and fresh. He read her feelings so well she didn't have to speak. He gave her whatever her body wanted and enjoyed everything she gave him in return. They loved to take their time when they made love, exploring each other with kisses and caresses, and when they finished he let her rest her head on his chest for as long as she wanted.

Over time, their intimacy lost some of the excitement but it more than made up for that with the way they'd grown to know each other's most intimate feelings. The two of them making love became like drinking a cup of coffee. Taylor knew exactly what to expect, no surprises there, but when she made love to Kyle, everything within her mind and body woke up and she felt wonderful.

Yet she had some doubts. It had been a long time for her to be with one person.

Chapter Eight

2022

After Susie called from the market, Taylor stepped toward the front door. "We shouldn't keep her waiting too long."

It surprised Kyle when she said *we*.

They walked to the boathouse and untied the Chris-Craft. The beautiful wooden 1968 Grand Prix was still in great shape. His grandfather had bought it from Susie's mother and had kept up with it himself. After Kyle inherited the boat, he stored it at Bridge Marina every winter and had the people there go over it before they put it back in the water. He also had someone check that the upholstery and the wood were kept in the finest shape.

The reason Kyle was so careful with the boat had to do with Susie's father, Scott. The man had been a Master Wood Carver. Scott Walsh made his living selling real estate and insurance but his *art* was carving. He built the fireplace mantel and carved the beautiful edging in its front and sides. He also carved the duck decoys displayed on the high shelves in the living room. Scott would never have been happy with a boat made of anything other than finely finished wood.

Scott used to tell anyone who would listen how he was giving new life to the material he worked with. The way he died was a horrible twist of fate. When that tree fell, the material Scott loved killed him.

Kyle backed the boat out of the boathouse and kept going until they were clear of his long dock. He spun the wheel, shifted to forward, and headed around the island, still at a slow speed. He felt a steady breeze on his face and for a moment wished he was taking Taylor for a sail in his Thistle instead of bringing her to meet Susie.

When Kyle's work required him to be alone with female colleagues Taylor would often make snide comments about the women, especially if he had to travel with someone to one of the other hotels in the chain. Kyle wasn't immune to the jealousy bug, so he understood her. When he sensed Taylor feeling insecure, he would reassure her she was everything he needed.

Yet Susie wasn't just a woman he worked with. She was someone he had thought about for decades. They were only thirteen when they last knew each other but feelings were always there. Maybe it was puppy love or maybe his first real crush. Whatever it was, he'd wanted to be around her every day back then and had suffered when they were forced apart.

Kyle pushed on the throttle and glanced over at Taylor in her zebra-striped bathing suit top and cutoff jeans. As the boat picked up speed, Taylor held her head high and let the wind blow her loose hair. She had grown used to riding in an open boat since moving in with him on the island. She looked beautiful.

He liked the fact that Susie had stepped back into his life. Susie was delicate and graceful but also powerful. Her eyes marked her good looks, like streaks of blue lightning in a hailstorm. Taylor had a simple beauty like a young fawn but every time he thought he knew her well she would surprise him. That was nice but somewhat dangerous.

As the boat approached the market, Kyle could see Susie waiting for them. She was wearing light blue shorts with a white trim that matched her white tank top. The blue would match her eyes when she removed her sunglasses. She and Taylor both had beautiful legs. He sighed. He would help Susie with her mother's last request but he needed to be careful.

Taylor turned her gaze to Kyle. He was the best-looking man she'd ever dated, especially with the wind blowing his spiky hair. He looked gorgeous in a black t-shirt that was so tight it could have been sewn on. She didn't want to lose Kyle's arms, his shoulders, and his deep-set eyes just because Susie was new.

Susie had recognized the boat her father once owned as soon as it appeared from around the island. The chance of another antique wooden boat heading toward Main Lake Market at that exact moment was almost zero.

Her dad had loved wood. She remembered the small statuettes he carved and gave away to friends and business acquaintances. The boat wasn't his creation but the beauty of its wood was the reason he had purchased it and why he had taken such good care of it.

When the boat was closer, she recognized Kyle and soon realized he'd brought his girlfriend with him. Susie hoped Taylor would not argue against allowing her to search their house.

They pulled up to the dock in front of the gas pumps even though they weren't there to buy fuel. Kyle held onto the dock to keep the boat from shifting while Taylor took Susie's purse, then held her hand as she stepped, first on the back seat, then the floor. Taylor also held Susie's upper arm, ostensibly to give her extra support but actually to feel if her arm was as firm as it looked. Her arm was not as solid as Kyle's but in much better shape than most of the women Taylor had known.

One minute Taylor didn't want Susie anywhere close to Kyle. The next minute she wouldn't mind if the woman hung around for a while. Perhaps it would be nice to have someone new to talk to, especially someone who looks fabulous in a white tank top. Yet Susie could cause a lot of problems if Taylor wasn't careful. Taylor felt as if she was being battered by waves in a hurricane.

Susie nodded to them both. "Thank you for picking me up."

Kyle started toward Halsey Island.

Susie leaned toward Taylor. "I assume Kyle told you about my mom's last wish."

"He did." Taylor paused. "I'm sorry to hear about her passing."

"Thank you. I don't understand this deathbed request of hers but I'm going to follow through with it. A promise is a promise."

"I don't think you'll have to search much."

"You don't? Why is that?"

"I know where the shoe is."

Kyle slowed the boat and turned to look at Taylor, his eyes wide. "You do?"

"Yes. I saw it a couple of months back when I was looking through a closet in your parents' room. I was thinking of storing some boxes there and wondered what was on the shelves."

"Why didn't you tell me?"

"I didn't remember it at first. Then, when the memory came back to me, I wanted to tell you and Susie at the same time. That's why I insisted I go with you to pick her up."

Susie was breathless. "That's wonderful. You're sure these are the shoes Kyle saw?"

"It's one shoe, but it fits his description, high-heeled with silver glitter. And Ginger Rogers' name is written on it."

"Great!" Kyle said.

Susie shook her head. "But Mom said shoes, not shoe."

"Maybe she misspoke. When I saw her at your party all those years ago, she was holding a single shoe. I told you that."

"She did not misspeak. She clearly said shoes." Susie rushed her words.

"There was also a note in the box." Taylor looked at Kyle then Susie. "I left it in there along with the shoe."

"What does it say?" Kyle asked.

"Don't throw this shoe away—ever."

Susie felt a breath catch in her chest. "That's it? No explanation?"

"Nope." Taylor paused. "But Nancy signed it. That's another reason I'm sure it's one of the shoes your mom wanted you to find."

Susie looked at Kyle. "Did you know about this?"

"No. I would have told you if I did." He rubbed his forehead. "Maybe my father or my mother knew, but they never mentioned anything to me, not even when I called them and told them what you were looking for." He narrowed his eyes. "I had no interest in going through the stuff in that closet. I just figured everything there belonged to them and they would tell me if they wanted something."

"Let's get back," Taylor suggested, "so I can show you what I found. We can talk after that. I'll help in any way I can."

Kyle pushed on the throttle and pointed the Chris-Craft toward his island home.

When he arrived, he pulled the boat into the boathouse. Susie and Taylor reached out for the dock to help him tie up. After they secured the boat, they headed to the main house and went inside.

Taylor ran straight upstairs, presumably to the main bedroom closet where she said she found the shoe. Kyle expected Susie to follow, but she stopped as soon as she entered the house. Her hand flew to her chest.

"It hasn't changed." Susie's voice rose in pitch. "This room looks exactly the way it did when I lived here."

She was right. Neither his grandfather nor he had changed anything about the place. They had even kept the furniture.

Her eyes widened as she stepped further into the living room. "Oh, how wonderful. You kept the white stag over the mantel."

The deer head over the fireplace was not white, but Kyle knew what Susie meant. The white stag was from the games they had played when they pretended to be characters from *The Lion, the Witch and the Wardrobe*. Kyle was always Peter. Susie switched back and forth between Susan and the White Witch, depending on her mood.

Susie spun around and laughed as if she'd just won the lottery. "Tell me, Kyle. Tell me you kept the wardrobe."

He nodded, although her comment confused him. Susie seemed more excited to see the place where they had played their Narnia games than she was to see the shoe she was seeking. She ran to the stairs and headed up. She had to be going to the bedroom Kyle now shared with Taylor.

Sure enough, Kyle found Susie upstairs in his bedroom, standing in front of the white wardrobe. The doors were open, and she seemed to be studying their clothing. Taylor and he both used closets in other rooms for most of their things but they each used half the wardrobe for items they would wear often. Most of the items weren't embarrassing but Taylor had a silky, yellow nightgown that laced up both sides.

Susie reached for the smooth fabric and smiled. "Not much material in this one, is there?"

Kyle shook his head. "No, but that's what makes it special."

Taylor's sleepwear was a code between her and Kyle. On evenings when Taylor was feeling intimate she would say, "I'm going to wear yellow tonight." When that happened Kyle would know to take a shower before he went to bed. Sometimes she wouldn't say anything but would put the gown on before she slipped in beside him. On those days Kyle knew she wanted sex even if he hadn't showered. It was a special gown, the only one Taylor hung up rather than folding.

Taylor wouldn't be pleased to know Susie had placed her hands on the gown but that didn't matter as much to Kyle as his own feelings. He didn't think of Taylor at that moment. He thought of lying next to Susie.

"Remember what we did here?" Susie said. "How we used to pretend we were going to Narnia then we would step inside and close the doors. Sometimes we stood in there, side by side, in the dark, for what seemed like hours. Remember that?"

"I do."

"Things were so much simpler back then."

He crossed his arms. "Yes they were and we might complicate things even further if Taylor catches us here, talking about spending time together in the dark."

Susie sighed. "I suppose you're right."

"He is." Kyle turned to see Taylor in the doorway. She was smiling, but it was a hard smile. She stared at Susie who was still fingering the smooth material.

"Are you here for the shoe, or not?" Taylor asked through clenched teeth.

Susie cleared her throat. "Sorry." She turned to hang Taylor's gown back in the wardrobe. "I couldn't resist seeing my old room again." She turned back toward Taylor who was holding a shoe box. "I have many memories here."

Taylor shook her head and turned to Kyle. "Do you want to see this?"

Kyle took the box and pulled out the shoe. "This is it. This is the shoe I saw your mother holding. And look." He moved to Susie. "Do you see the signature? It's hard to read but look at the huge G and R. It has to be Ginger Rogers' autograph."

Taylor took the shoebox back and pulled out a piece of paper. "Here's the note." She handed it to Susie.

"It's my mother's handwriting. This is real." She looked at the note and read, "Don't throw this shoe away—ever."

Kyle handed the shoe to Susie. "Let's go downstairs and talk."

"That's an idea," Taylor said, turning abruptly and stepping into the hall.

Kyle tilted his head and raised his eyebrows as he looked at Susie. He followed Taylor and Susie followed him.

Taylor led Kyle and Susie downstairs and out onto the porch. At the far end, there were two wicker chairs, and a settee positioned around a low, round table with a glass top. Taylor walked straight to the settee and sat on one side. Kyle knew he had better sit next to her or things would get even more complicated. He took his seat while Susie sat in the closest chair.

Instead of offering drinks or snacks, something Taylor did when they had a guest, she said, "Kyle, please fix me a gin and tonic and get something for Susie. I'd like to speak with her alone."

Susie straightened her back. "A drink sounds nice. I'd love a glass of white wine if you have an open bottle."

Chapter Nine

Taylor could feel the tension as she and Susie sat watching a couple of outboard runabouts race in the open water below them. The two women waited without speaking while Kyle left the porch. Taylor broke the silence once she heard the screen door shut. "I admire you." Her voice was quiet and flat. "I want you to know that." Taylor could see Susie's jaw drop.

"You do?" Susie looked down then back up again. "Why?"

Taylor laughed. "I should have expected that reaction."

"I'm sorry. You looked upset, so I thought…" Susie's voice trailed off.

"Kyle talks about you a lot."

"It's been a long time since we last saw each other. We were children."

"You stayed on his mind over all these years. I should feel threatened but I don't. Kyle loves the image of the thirteen-year-old Susie you once were, not the woman you've become."

"And that's why you admire me? Because I've grown old?"

"No." Taylor sat up straight. "It's because you're honoring your mother's last wish. Your loyalty is beautiful." What she was saying was true, not the whole truth by any means, but true nonetheless. She leaned toward Susie and lowered her voice. "And you are not old. You're in your prime and attractive. Like I said, I should feel threatened but I don't." Taylor rolled her eyes upward, took in a breath, then looked back at Susie. "I can tell you aren't happy about only finding a single shoe."

Susie's eyes flashed. "She said *shoes* twice!"

The screen door slammed, causing Taylor to turn. She saw Kyle walking to them with drinks in both hands. He must have kicked the door shut to make it so loud.

"Here are the drinks for you two ladies." He held the glasses out as he stepped toward the table. "I'll be right back. I'm going to get a beer."

Susie took a sip of her drink. They sat in silence until the door slammed again.

Taylor slid over on the settee and leaned toward Susie. "Did you spend much time on this porch when the house was yours?"

"No. About all I did was run across it to spend time out on the dock—lots of time. My mom and dad used to sit up here and yell down at me if they saw me doing anything wrong."

"Like what?"

Susie pursed her lips. "The things kids do all the time, like running too close to the edge of the dock or swimming too soon after eating."

"It was good they watched you so closely."

"I guess so but they could have sat on the dock instead of way up here."

Taylor heard the screen door opening and shutting one more time and turned to see Kyle making his way back to them, holding a Stella Artois in his right hand. "It's a perfect day to enjoy the lake," he told the two women. Taylor nodded. It was sunny, and the breeze had picked up.

Kyle sat on the settee next to Taylor. He leaned forward so he could see around her as he spoke to Susie. "So what do you intend to do now?"

"I intend to find the other shoe but what you saw my mom doing at that party was my only clue. I'll have to think about my next step."

Taylor shrugged. "Somebody has it. I'm sure. Nobody would throw away something like that. The only reason to split the pair would be if they both have value alone. The other one is probably autographed also, and might have another note with it."

Susie was frowning but after Taylor spoke Susie smiled. "That means either Kyle's grandfather, his great-grandfather, my mother, or Ginger Rogers herself gave away the other part of this pair."

Kyle shook his head. "The people who knew Ginger Rogers or my great-grandfather will be gone by now."

"True. But my mother knew there were two shoes so the pair must have been split after she first saw them. I think we can concentrate on people who knew her. The people she was closest to were your parents. We could start there."

"I can call them tonight," Kyle said, reaching over Taylor to take Susie's hand. "And even if they don't know who has the shoe, they'll certainly know others we can ask."

Taylor felt her stomach harden as Kyle kept his clasp on Susie's hand. She wanted to pull them apart, but she swallowed her irritation and put both her hands on top of theirs. She pushed them down to her lap. Kyle and Susie quickly pulled back as Taylor said, "Remember we're in this together—all three of us."

* * *

Taylor and Kyle brought Susie back to Main Lake Market in their Chris-Craft. She waved goodbye as they took off, then walked up to where she had left her car.

Learning why her mother had made such an odd last request was foremost on her heart and now they had a plan. Susie was excited but knew she had to be careful. She had not seen Kyle in decades and they were children the last time they were together. Yet yesterday, when Taylor brought her up to him on the porch of her old house, she had felt her stomach flutter and today, when he expressed concern and willingness to help, her whole body seemed to tingle. Kyle seemed clueless about her feelings but Taylor seemed to sense the heat. The last thing Susie wanted was to be part of a love triangle.

What she needed was some time with another man. When she got back to her apartment, she called the Chester Theater, reserved a couple of tickets for that night's presentation of *The Dresser*, and called Danny.

Susie was a little nervous but felt calm as soon as he picked up the phone. "I need something fun to do and I thought of you. Have you seen *The Dresser?*"

"I saw the film."

"Not the same thing."

"I know."

"They're doing a production of it at the Chester Theatre. I know this is last minute but the show's supposed to be good. I've got tickets reserved for tonight and I was hoping you could join me for dinner and the show."

"That sounds nice."

"Great. My treat, of course, since I'm the one asking."

"That's not necessary."

"I think it is. Let's meet at The Randolph Diner at six. Sound good? We can talk about why I should pick up the check over a glass of wine."

He gave in and let her pay. The food was good, and the play was great, although Susie felt she would have been a better choice to play Irene. Her friend Deb got the part and didn't seem sweet enough for the role. Susie could do sweet better than Candace Cameron Bure. She would go back to auditioning after she found the other shoe.

After the show, Danny and she went to her apartment. That part of the evening wasn't perfect, but the sex was good enough to get her mind to focus on Kyle as a resource rather than an attractive man. She would go out with Danny again and next time he would pay.

In the morning, after Danny left, she called Kyle to ask if he'd spoken to his parents. She felt her stomach tighten as she dialed the phone.

He answered after four rings. "I talked to them yesterday afternoon. Dad didn't understand what was so important about a Ginger Rogers autograph. His actual words were, 'A Ginger Rogers shoe isn't anything like a Honus Wagner baseball card.'" Kyle laughed before adding, "He didn't think it could be worth more than a few hundred dollars at most. But he remembered it."

"Just the one?"

"Yes. He saw an autographed shoe after my grandfather passed—when he was going through his father's stuff. Mom remembered nothing about the shoes but my mom and your mom were in a group of close friends who got together every couple of weeks and would often go on vacations together. She talked about visiting your mother at the island house when your family owned it—before either of us were born. They used to canoe together from Halsey to the Glasser post office in Henderson Bay. She said they would paddle over, pick up the mail, paddle back, and talk the entire time. That's when she remembered your mother telling her about things that bothered her and things she enjoyed—normal girl talk if you know what I mean."

"Did she remember anything in particular?"

"Yes, she did—not from way back but from later when your parents were trying to start their family. Nancy was having trouble getting pregnant. Mom said she was quite emotional about the struggle. But you're here now so they must have gotten through that problem eventually."

"She never mentioned it."

"Is there any reason she would have?"

Susie scratched her chin. "I suppose not but she had some traits that don't match mine. Both my parents had brown eyes. My father had a blue-eyed brother, so I always figured they both had the recessive gene. There is another possibility. You don't suppose I was adopted?"

"Wouldn't they have told you if you were?"

"I would think so but—maybe not. I could see my mother putting off the talk until I was older and never getting around to it."

There was an awkward pause before Kyle said, "I could call my mother again and ask her."

"Ask her if I was adopted?"

"Yes. They saw each other all the time back then. She would have noticed if your mother suddenly had a child without showing any signs of being pregnant."

Susie pondered Kyle's suggestion. It made sense. "Could I talk to her?"

"Of course, just remember they're in Stockholm and there's a six-hour difference in time so you have to be a little careful about when you call. Now is a good time. It's quarter to nine here so it will be quarter to three there."

"All right. Give me her number. I'll talk to her and call you back when we're done."

It took a little time for the call to go through. This was the first international call Susie had ever made. She thought that could be the problem.

When Susie finally heard Mary's smooth voice she felt as if a whirlpool had pulled her back to her childhood, even though Mary had picked up a slight Swedish accent. "I'm sorry to hear about your mother, Susie. Losing a parent is one of the worst things we go through in our lives, all of us. But this has brought you and Kyle back together, which is one good thing."

Susie's stomach rolled. She pressed her free hand against her midsection, the phone still to her ear. "Silver lining?"

"I suppose that's what I'm saying although it sounds horrible when you put it that way."

Suzie wondered if she should have let Kyle make the call.

"What I'm trying to say," Mary continued in a low, steady voice, "is that you were the daughter I never had. Then you were gone. I should have tried to stay in touch."

Susie looked at the floor. "It wouldn't have done any good. My father died, and we had to sell the lake house. All these things were wrong with my life. I didn't want to see anyone, not even Kyle or you."

"Especially not us, since we were the ones living in your house."

"That was one thing, but believe me there was more to it than that. Remember, I loved you both—still do."

"That's sweet of you to say."

"It's true."

"I hope so but what can I do for you? I already told Kyle I don't remember the shoes you're looking for. This all seems strange to me."

Susie decided not to start with the adoption question. Instead, she dove right into the main reason she'd called. "Kyle told you this was Mom's last request, didn't he?"

"Yes, but I still don't understand."

"Neither do I. I expect I will once I have the complete pair. My mom had to be serious about this. Asking me to find them would not have been her idea of a joke."

"You're right. So what do you need?"

"I need names. I hope you remember the group you two hung out with when you were in your twenties."

"I know the women you're thinking of and I can name a couple of them." Mary paused for a moment. "I remember Lisa Thomas clearly because she lost her daughter when the girl was an infant. Sudden Death Syndrome is what they said. Lisa had some trouble with depression after that and last I knew she was still suffering but that was decades ago. She and Theresa Robinson had houses on the east shore of the lake.

"I knew Theresa better than I knew Lisa, although I've lost touch with both of them over the years. Theresa was sweet and always upbeat. Her husband ran for mayor of Mount Arlington one time. Your mother and I helped them address campaign letters. He lost, but he won a position on the borough council the following year."

Susie's legs were getting tired, but this was stuff she wanted to hear. She switched her phone to her other ear, then stepped to a chair and sat down. "Any others?"

"There were a couple of others but I can't remember their names. I wish I could be of more help."

"You've given me a place to start, which is what I needed. Thank you so much."

"I'll get back in touch if any other names come to me."

Before Mary could hang up Susie said, "There is one other thing I wanted to ask."

"What's that?"

"Do you know if I was adopted?"

"What makes you ask that?"

"My blue eyes."

Mary paused, causing Susie to ask, "Are you still there?"

"I am." She paused again for a shorter time. "At first, when I saw how blue your eyes were, I wondered how that happened. I thought they would turn brown as you got older but they never did and after a few years I just stopped thinking about it."

"My parents never mentioned an adoption?"

"They said nothing. But although your mother told us she was pregnant, she never looked like she was. She wore loose clothing as she got close to her due date but still looked thin and she hadn't changed much when she brought you home."

"You didn't visit her in the hospital?"

"You were born in New York. Nancy wanted a doctor who worked in the city. She told us not to come—said it would be too much of a hassle. I had planned to visit her, but I figured if she didn't want us, I wouldn't go."

"So you know no more than I do?"

"I guess so."

"Well, Mary, thank you so much for talking to me. I enjoyed this conversation."

"Me too. Don't wait so long next time. It's a joy to speak with you and I'm so glad you're back in touch with Kyle."

Susie called Kyle after she said goodbye to his mother. The first thing she told him was, "It was good to hear her voice again. I've missed her, not as much as I've missed you but still..."

"Was she helpful?"

"I'm still confused about the idea of an adoption but she gave me a couple of names, which was all I'd hoped for. You'd already told me the shoes meant nothing to her."

"Names are good, right?"

"She knew them a long time ago. I might have trouble getting in touch."

"I'll help if I can."

"Thank you. If I can find one, that one should help me reach the other and maybe give me names your mother couldn't recall."

"So where do you start?"

Susie cleared her throat. "I'll start with Google. If that doesn't work I'll try other ways, voter records maybe? If I can find either of them still living in the area, I'll head to her door. That's what I did with you and that worked." Susie gave Kyle a moment for that comment to sink in. "I realize there are problems with this plan. I don't even know if the women are still alive. But this is all I've got, so it's what I intend to do."

Susie heard some muffled sounds and was sure Kyle was holding his hand over the phone. When he started speaking clearly he said, "Let us know when you're going to the first home. Taylor and I want to join you."

"Taylor and you?"

"Yes. I'm interested in this because it involves my mother."

"And Taylor because...?"

"Because she's interested in me."

Susie thought she should suggest bringing Danny along to make this a double date but she was worried Kyle might take her seriously.

Chapter Ten

Finding information about Lisa Thomas was possible through real estate records and some old articles in local newspapers. Susie called Kyle at work the next day to explain what she discovered. "Lisa's mother moved in with her after her child died and her marriage broke up. They lived in the home she got from the divorce settlement until five years ago when her mother died. Lisa stayed in the house—alone. Her home is a block from the lake, toward the southern part, near Ingram Cove."

Kyle made a soft humming sound before asking, "Do you know anything else about her?"

"Not much. She doesn't seem to have a presence on social media. I can't find her on Facebook, Instagram, Twitter, or LinkedIn. That says something about her, I guess."

"That she doesn't like computers?"

"It says more than that." Susie looked up at the ceiling. "Somebody would have mentioned her in at least one post if she attended church or was involved in most anything else. I think Lisa's a loner."

"You're thinking she never got over the loss of her child?"

"That would be understandable, wouldn't it?"

"Maybe."

"Either way, Lisa might remember the shoes. I intend to drop by her home tomorrow."

Susie heard Taylor's voice in the background. Kyle said something but Susie couldn't understand what. She thought he had his palm over the phone.

"Taylor wants us to go to Lisa's together."

"The three of us?"

"Tomorrow is Sunday so we don't have to be at work."

"All right. Do you want me to pick you up at Bridge Marina?"

"No. Taylor wants you to come for dinner tonight and to spend the night here. She says it will be fun and while we're together, we can plan how to approach Lisa Thomas. She's excited about this search."

"Oh. That's a surprise." Susie wasn't sure she wanted Taylor's input on how to search but she loved the idea of spending a night in her old home, even if Kyle would sleep in another room with Taylor. "What time?"

"Call me from Main Lake Market around five. I'll pick you up."

Five was a good time. It meant Susie had most of the afternoon to do some shopping. She needed to pick up a bottle of wine and while she was out, she would also buy something special to wear. The image of Taylor in a bikini was burned into her mind. That woman had also looked great in the striped top and cutoffs she wore the day after the party. Someone who looked that good could draw all the attention in a room and Susie didn't want that. She wanted Kyle to pay attention to her.

Susie would buy a new outfit and a nice pajama set. It was likely Taylor would eat breakfast without changing. Susie had to do the same.

* * *

The smell of a pork tenderloin Taylor had in the oven filled the house. The aroma made Kyle hungry enough to eat before Susie arrived but he didn't. Taylor had been busy all day, cooking for the last hour and shopping before that. Kyle had walked in and out of the kitchen often enough to see she was putting together a sauce with blackberries, raspberries, blueberries, and jalapeno pepper. There were plenty of other ingredients on the counter but those were enough to make his mouth water.

"Are you coming?" Kyle asked Taylor after Susie rang.

"Can't now. You pick her up while I finish here."

Kyle walked out the front way and down the hill. He untied the Chris-Craft, backed it out of the boathouse, and headed around the island. Susie had probably been waiting at least ten minutes by the time he was approaching Main Lake Market but she knew the lake well enough to understand.

When he was close enough he was surprised to see she was wearing a dress. This was the lake. Why wasn't she in shorts or jeans? He had on khaki shorts and a black t-shirt. Maybe he'd given her the wrong impression when he'd asked her to join him and Taylor for dinner.

The dress was light blue, a color that would have matched her eyes if her sunglasses weren't covering them. Even as a child, he couldn't get enough of those eyes. He was eager to get her home so she would remove the glasses.

He grabbed her hand and helped her into the boat. "You look good." Kyle pushed the boat away from the dock and took the driver's seat.

Susie sat on the bench seat beside him. "Thank you. I'm going to wear this tomorrow. I wanted something that looks pretty but conservative, something that will help Lisa trust me."

The dress had two layers, a sleeveless shift with a sheer layer over it. The sheer layer had cap sleeves and a skirt that was light enough to wave gently when she moved. He wanted her to stand and spin but he would never ask her to do that even when they were back on dry land.

He nodded. "That should work." It was a beautiful look, gorgeous. He didn't know what else to say, so he pushed on the throttle and headed back to the island. The wind blew over the windshield. He glanced at Susie's lap and saw her skirt fluttering. She held it down, and he averted his eyes.

They pulled into the boathouse, tied up the Chris-Craft, and headed to the house. As they climbed the hill, most of their conversation was about how well-kept the house was, especially the bushes around the front porch.

"I'm glad so much of this house is the same as it was when we owned it. I remember hiding behind those large azaleas when I was five or six. My parents would sit on the porch and I could hear everything they said."

Kyle grinned. "My grandfather didn't want to change the yard, and neither did I. This entire house is special."

"You must have worked hard to keep it looking so nice."

He walked a little taller.

Taylor greeted them when they entered the house. Kyle was more surprised by her outfit than he had been by what Susie was wearing. Taylor had on a black halter dress, embellished with pictures of fist-size sunflowers in groups of one, two, or three. The dress had no back and a skirt that reached less than halfway down her thigh. When he'd left, she'd been wearing her cutoff jeans with a yellow t-shirt, along with an old apron for cooking.

Kyle had never seen that dress before. Taylor must have stopped at a dress store before she shopped for the dinner ingredients.

Taylor served garlic cauliflower and a pea salad as sides with the pork loin. She was an excellent cook but most of her meals were simpler than this. She set the table with the china she'd brought with her when she moved in with Kyle. This was the first time she'd used those dishes since the time they invited her cousin and his family for a day at the lake.

Kyle did not know why she was making everything so fancy. When she'd first asked Susie to spend the night at their house, he had expected hamburgers and corn on the cob served on paper plates. Although he didn't understand why Taylor was doing this, he appreciated her effort. Taylor was treating Susie like royalty even though she was his friend, not hers. That was sweet. Susie ate well and smiled a lot so she must have been comfortable.

They went through a bottle of Pinot Blanc, opened a second, and were close to finishing that one. Kyle was on his second glass which meant he'd drunk less than either of the women. They must have had three glasses each, at least.

Susie had mentioned she loved how they'd kept the house the way she'd known it when she was a child. For that reason, Kyle wanted to center the dinner conversation on the past. He brought up a time they had gone with their fathers to the lake house in January when they were both six years old. "We parked by The Windlass and crossed on the ice."

Susie held her hand to her heart and sighed. "Oh yes! Snow covered the yard. It was so deep we had trouble making it up the hill to the house. I kept slipping and every time you would hold out your hand to help me back to my feet." Her voice turned bubbly as she said, "That was nice."

Kyle leaned toward Susie. "Remember how our fathers went inside to start a fire while we built a couple of competing ice forts." He laughed. "The forts ended up being two walls we could duck behind as we threw snowballs at each other."

"Yes. Yes. Then my father came out and joined me, making the battle two against one."

"Until *my* father came out and joined my side."

Taylor mumbled something Kyle couldn't understand. He turned to her and noticed her face was turning slightly red. She raised her voice saying, "Can we talk about Lisa Thomas?"

Susie put her hand on Kyle's arm. "That snowball fight went on for more than an hour when we declared a truce. We went inside, had hot chocolate, and sat by the fire."

Kyle leaned toward Susie. "Remember how our clothes were soaked? You had some old clothes you could change into but I had to put on your father's shirt and wrap myself in a blanket." He paused. "I was embarrassed."

Taylor reached across the table and grabbed Kyle's other arm. "We don't know much about Lisa but we know enough to prepare to meet her tomorrow. We know she's depressed."

"We don't even know that," Susie said, changing her focus from Kyle to Taylor. "It's been years since she lost the child—decades even."

Neither of the women had reacted to Kyle's admission of being embarrassed and the conversation had moved on. He cleared his throat.

Taylor frowned at Kyle, then turned back to Susie. "Tell me all you know about Lisa."

"I know she's had a rough life. I believe the loss of her child and the breakup of her marriage hit her so hard she had no choice but to convince her mother to move in with her. She needed to go back to living the protected life she'd had as a child. After her mother died, she stayed in that house."

"You're sure about all that?"

"No. This is all conjecture based on what is and is not on the internet. I could be way off base." Susie shrugged. "I can't find any sign that Lisa has hobbies or is involved with clubs or a church. All I know for sure is that she lives alone. My feeling is the loss of her child and the breakup of her marriage put her in such a serious downward spiral she never recovered. I doubt she has many friends."

"So what does this mean?"

"It means, we'll probably have trouble talking to her. We'll have to be careful but persistent. If she cracks the door open and we shout, 'We're here about Ginger's shoes, she'll run for the hills.'"

Taylor rubbed her jaw. "Well…Can we bring her something?"

"What do you have in mind?"

"I was thinking food. I could fill a small Corning Ware with leftovers from tonight's dinner."

"Not a bad idea."

"We can tell her we're looking into people who were close to your mother, making sure they're OK. We can even say looking for her old friends was your mother's request. Indirectly, it was. How else could you look for the shoes if you didn't start with her friends?"

Susie sucked her teeth. "That's great. You, Taylor, are brighter than you look."

Taylor laughed. "I don't know how to take that."

Susie reached for the wine and emptied the last of the second bottle into Taylor's glass. "I meant it as a compliment."

Taylor loved a good mystery and there were plenty of reasons to think this was an intriguing one: a deathbed wish, a film celebrity from the nineteen thirties, and, of course, Susie's gorgeous eyes. Taylor's heart had raced when Susie used the word *compliment*. She cared what Susie thought of her and hoped this friend of Kyle's would allow her to help with the search for the shoe.

Taylor raised her wineglass and said, "To Ginger's other shoe. May we have success in our search."

Susie raised her glass and added, "And in the process may we discover why my mother wanted us to find it."

"I'll drink to both toasts," Kyle said, raising his beer.

For dessert, Taylor served a Tiramisu Layer Cake she had picked up at the Neverland Bake Shoppe on River Styx Road. The coffee and cocoa flavors of the cake complemented the rich dark coffee she had brewed.

Kyle was responsible for doing the dishes since Taylor had cooked the meal. He stood and began clearing the table. Taylor offered Susie a glass of Kahlua, which, after the Tiramisu and cup of Joe, might have been too much coffee for most people.

Susie gave Taylor a thumbs up. "I'm a huge caffeine fan. This is the perfect end to a wonderful meal."

Taylor touched Susie on her shoulder. "Let's move to the porch while we enjoy our drinks."

Susie took her drink and followed Taylor. As they stepped through the front door Taylor told Susie she liked her dress.

Susie smiled. "Thank you. I intend to wear it tomorrow."

"You look nice in it." Taylor noticed that Susie's perfume had a slight aroma of something floral mixed with chocolate. She liked it.

"You look nice in yours, too," Susie replied. "And very sexy."

"Is that another one of your compliments?"

"I intended it that way."

They both laughed.

"I'll wear something casual tomorrow when we visit Lisa. That will keep her attention on you."

They sat in two wicker rocking chairs, sipping on the drinks and looking out over the lake. This being a Saturday evening, there was some activity on the water. It was still light enough for the motor boats to be running full speed. For a few minutes, the two women sat in silence watching a couple of kayaks circling the island close to the end of Kyle's dock.

Taylor was the first to speak. "Tell me something about your life here before you had to sell the house."

"Things weren't all that different from what they are now. The lake was more peaceful with fewer boats and none as powerful as some you see nowadays. But it still has an aura about it of people in tune with nature."

"Come on, Susie. I already know that stuff. Tell me about your life, about one or two events that happened to you alone."

"You really want to hear about me?"

"I do. Tell me something that affected you but didn't involve Kyle."

"All right. Here's something that was traumatic. When I was six years old, my mom and dad wanted to go out for dinner and dancing at a club near River Styx Road. They hired a teenager to babysit for me. I think she was 17 and lived over in East Shore Estates but I'm not sure I remember that right. Her name was

Miriam, but I called her Mimi. Mom and Dad didn't know her but they knew her family through the yacht club. Mimi seemed nice, clean-cut, and all of that. She made a phone call after my parents had been gone for about a half hour. When she got off the phone, she told me she wanted to take a boat ride and I had to go with her. My dad had picked her up so she didn't have her own boat. The plan was to borrow my dad's Chris-Craft. That's what she did, and she dragged me along. Told me I had to listen to her because she was in charge. We picked up Josh, her boyfriend, from a dock in Byram Bay and he took over driving the boat my father loved. I was so scared.

"He drove to the center of Indian Harbor and shut the engine off. He and Mimi began to make out. Although I'm certain it was romantic for the two of them with the stars and the sound of ripples against the side of the boat, it was traumatic for six-year-old me. I knew what kissing was but not much else. Since I was sitting in the back of the boat, I couldn't see what was happening after they slid down on the bench seat but I could hear them. Mimi said, 'Susie is back there.' And I heard Josh reply, 'She can't see us.' There were more sounds, mostly groans from both of them until they stopped, Josh first then Mimi a short time later. They both sat up without looking. After they straightened their clothes, Mimi turned to me and said, 'Don't tell anyone about this, understand?' I nodded and said, 'I promise.' But I *didn't* understand and that was the problem."

Taylor shook her head slowly. "Wow. That's fucked up, but memories often change from what we saw to what we think we saw."

"You think I made this up?"

"You were six and in the back of the boat. Isn't it possible you think you saw more than what happened?"

"I know what they were doing."

Taylor pulled in a breath and slowly released it.

Susie stood. "I know children can remember things differently from the way they happened."

Taylor reached over and took her hand. "So can adults."

"I *am* sure about two things. I was six, and they had their hands all over each other while I was in the back seat of this boat. They weren't just kissing."

Taylor shook her head. "You're missing my point." She looked straight at Susie. "You can't count on anyone remembering every exact detail, even after a short time."

"So?"

"So maybe your mom did not say *shoes*. Maybe she said *shoe*."

Susie pulled her hand from Taylor's grip and tightened her fists. "I know what Mimi and Josh were doing and I know what my mom said. Let's go in the house. Kyle must be wondering where we are."

"Finish this first," Taylor said, handing Susie her drink. They gulped down the remaining Kahlua in their glasses.

They went inside and found him in the kitchen, finishing up the dishes.

Taylor suggested they play a game of Trivial Pursuit. After Susie admitted she'd never played, Kyle suggested he and Taylor compete. Susie could help them both with the answers. "And we'll use the Silver Screen Edition," he told her. "With your interest in acting, you probably know a great deal about films."

"Not as much as you might think but that sounds fun."

After Taylor set the board up she offered more drinks. Kyle asked for a beer but Susie begged off alcohol and switched to tea. They threw the die to decide who went first. Kyle beat Taylor's three with his five and made his move.

Susie read the question that matched the color he'd landed on, which was: *What kind of creature was the Creature from the Black Lagoon?* After Kyle failed to answer correctly, he told a story of something else he'd shared with Susie. It was from a time when they were in second grade. The teacher had told the children to go on a shape hunt in their classroom. Kyle cried because he didn't know the name of any shape other than a circle. Susie saw he was upset and helped him. She showed him stars and triangles. She taught him the difference between rectangles and squares. He said he would always be grateful to her for helping him through that day.

Taylor waited patiently for Kyle to finish his story before she threw the die and made her move. She had grown weary of stories about Susie and Kyle when they were together.

Halfway into the second round of the game, Susie announced she was feeling tired. She excused herself and started toward the stairway.

Taylor stood to follow. "You're in the master bedroom facing the lake. I'll lay out a towel and washcloth for you in the bathroom."

When Susie got to the bedroom, she stripped out of the blue dress she had been wearing and hung it on a hanger. She looked it over to be sure she hadn't soiled it during the day. She hadn't, not even when she climbed in and out of the boat. Susie would be comfortable wearing it tomorrow to meet Lisa Thomas. She was glad Taylor had said she wouldn't be wearing her sunflower dress. It was pretty but a little too much to be meeting a recluse.

Susie took off her underwear and pulled on the blue nightgown she bought for this night. She went to where her dress was hanging and picked up the hem of her nightgown so she could compare the two. The nightgown was a little lighter, but both materials matched her eyes well. She felt she would look good at the breakfast table tomorrow and at Lisa's home.

She turned off the light and crawled into the bed, pulling the covers over her, even though it was a warm night. It was a little strange sleeping in this room. Her parents had slept in it. She'd always slept in the bedroom on the back side of the house, the one where Taylor and Kyle slept now. She wondered why they hadn't moved to the master bedroom but that was none of her business.

Susie fell asleep fairly quickly, perhaps from the wine and the Kahlua. It was a restless sleep, light enough that the sound of panting and groaning woke her. She sat up in the bed and saw it was a short time after midnight according to the clock on the dresser. The sounds were soft but enough to keep her awake, especially since Susie wondered if someone was hurt. She listened closely and could still hear the sounds. She got out of bed and cracked the door. There was a man's voice saying, "Oh…Ah…Oh." She stepped into the hall and tiptoed toward the other bedroom. It had to be Kyle and he could be in pain, although he sounded as if he was trying to muffle his voice. She heard Taylor say, "That's right. Yes. Yes." She was also trying to muffle her voice.

It wasn't pain. It was sex. They were having sex while she was trying to sleep in the room down the hall. Susie tiptoed back to the master bedroom, closed the door as quietly as possible, and got back into bed. She still couldn't sleep but now it was because she was angry. Taylor had invited her to spend the night, heard the story of what Mimi and Josh did when she was six years old, then decided it was fine to have noisy sex just a few yards away from where she was lying in bed, staring up at the dark ceiling. *Oh God*, she thought, *I hope tomorrow goes better than today.*

Chapter Eleven

As the sun rose, light spilled into the room through the window overlooking the woods behind the house. Kyle slipped out of bed, moving gently so as not to wake Taylor. He made it downstairs before he heard any stirring sounds from either Taylor or Susie. He went to the kitchen to get breakfast started. The plan was to make pancakes, pop some bread in the toaster, scramble a few eggs, and fry bacon. He would also put out a few boxes of cold cereal so the women could eat healthy if they chose to.

Taylor came into the kitchen while Kyle was cooking. She was still wearing the red silk nightgown she'd worn to bed. Last night was the first time in months they'd made love with her wearing something other than her yellow nightgown. Kyle had enjoyed the slick feel of Taylor's gown as he had pulled it over her head and off her arms. The smooth touch was almost enough to knock Susie out of his head.

Now that Taylor was in the light instead of the darkness of their bedroom he could see the material was as shiny as it had felt and he could appreciate how beautiful she was in it. The sight of her standing there, with her matching robe open and one side hanging down over her shoulder, filled him with more awe than a sunrise over the lake. Kyle woke to Taylor every day but still couldn't take his eyes off her. He had to be careful not to burn the pancakes. She stepped to him, gave him a light kiss, then asked if she could help with the breakfast.

"You could set the table, if you like, and get a pot of coffee going. Hopefully, Susie will be down pretty soon."

"Is this soon enough for you?" Susie said as she stepped into the kitchen.

Kyle spun to see her, and his jaw dropped. Except for the color of her gown, she and Taylor were dressed almost identically. Susie's nightgown and robe were also silk, but hers were light blue, matching her amazing eyes. There was also a white lace border along the edge of her neckline.

They were both gorgeous women. Taylor's hair was brown while Susie's was blond. Taylor's breasts were bigger, and she was shorter. Susie's skin was lighter and her legs were longer. Taylor's gown revealed more cleavage, but it was Susie's eyes that always stopped him in his tracks, even when they were children.

Taylor finished pouring water into the coffeemaker and turned it on. "We've got breakfast going here."

Susie smiled. "That's good. I'm starving."

Taylor closed her robe and tied the sash. "I'm looking forward to meeting Lisa today." She smiled at Susie. "Hopefully, the woman will tell you something that will help you find that shoe."

"I'm hoping for the same thing."

Kyle brought a plate of pancakes over to the table. "I'm not sure you made the right decision." He used the spatula to put a couple on her plate. "There's a good chance she won't appreciate us dropping by without calling ahead. It wouldn't surprise me if she slams the door in your face."

"I don't think she'll do that," Susie said.

"Just don't be disappointed if she does."

"You're such a pessimist, Kyle." Taylor reached for the coffee pot after it stopped gurgling. She poured a cup for each of them. "All we have to do is mention Susie's mother. Lisa will want to hear about her old friend."

Kyle narrowed his eyes. "If we get in her house, do we bring up the loss of her baby?"

"Why would we do that?" Taylor asked.

"Because Lisa knew Susie's mom before that tragedy affected her so badly."

Susie sat up straight. "We'll play it by ear but I insist on one thing. Both of you need to follow my lead, understand?"

Kyle and Taylor nodded.

When they were done with their breakfast, Kyle cleared the table while Taylor and Susie went back to their rooms to change.

* * *

Lisa's house was on a road that ran along its side. To get in people had to either walk up the drive and enter through the back door or up a set of steps onto a deck and enter through the front. The front faced the lake but was set back a distance from the waterfront. Other homes partially obstructed the lake from the deck but the view was still nice. Susie, Kyle, and Taylor went to the front door.

Susie knocked while Kyle and Taylor stood behind her. Taylor was dressed casually, as she had said she would. She wore jeans and a long-sleeved t-shirt with a floral print. Kyle was also wearing jeans with a black polo shirt. As she had planned, Susie was wearing the blue dress she'd had on the day before.

Susie looked around for a bell but finding none, she knocked on the door again. There was no answer, so she knocked a third and fourth time. Finally, she heard someone moving about until that person cracked open the door and peeked through the crack. All that was visible was one light blue eye, a small amount of gray hair, and wrinkled skin. Susie couldn't see enough of this person to know if this was a woman or a man.

"Who are you?" It was a woman's voice. She knew it was Lisa.

Susie leaned close to the door. "We need to talk to you."

The woman started to close the door until Taylor stepped forward and said, "This is Susie Walsh. Nancy Walsh's daughter. She's come to talk to you."

"Oh." The woman opened the door. "Nancy's daughter? That's strange. Please come in."

"You're Lisa?"

"Yes." She was a heavy woman with thick salt and pepper hair cut short except for her bangs. She wore an orange housedress with a white paisley pattern. Susie had expected her to be in her mid-fifties, but she looked a lot older. Her back was hunched and the skin on her neck was loose.

"Sit there," Lisa said. She held a silver, metal cane which she used to point toward a black vinyl couch. "Would you like tea?"

"None for me," Taylor told her as they walked by Lisa. "But I brought cake if you would like a slice." She held a box containing what was left of the Tiramisu they'd had the night before.

"No, thank you. I'm not hungry."

"No cake for me, either," Susie said, "or tea."

Kyle just shook his head.

Susie took a straight-back chair that was against a wall, brought it to the center of the room, and sat. Kyle picked a spot on the couch and Taylor sat beside him, setting the box with the cake on the coffee table.

After Lisa took a seat in a wingback chair Susie told her, "My mother died recently."

"I'm sorry to hear that."

"Thank you."

"It's hard to lose someone you love. My daughter died many years ago but I still miss her every day."

"I'm sorry for your loss, too. She must have been very special for you to carry her in your heart for so long."

"She was." Lisa nodded slowly. "But you didn't come here to tell me about your mother's death, did you?"

"We did, in a way. My mother made a deathbed wish and I'm trying to honor it. We're hoping you can help us with it."

Lisa raised her eyebrows. "I will if I can."

"She told me to find Ginger's shoes. I did not know what she meant, but I remembered Kyle seeing her with a dance shoe in her hands a long time ago. So I contacted him and we found one shoe at the old lake house where I spent my early childhood. He owns that house now."

"I noticed it while cleaning a closet," Taylor said. "In a box that had been there for years."

Susie was glad Taylor had said something, even if it wasn't important. She didn't want to be the only one speaking and Kyle had been as quiet as a fish since they'd entered the house.

"That's right," Susie told Lisa, "and Ginger Rogers had autographed the shoe Taylor found, so we were certain it was one of the pair we were looking for. Now the question is—who has the other shoe?"

Lisa shook her head but smiled. She looked at Susie, then Taylor, then back at Susie. "Maybe my story will help you. I'd love to tell it, if you will listen."

Chapter Twelve

Thirty-Seven Years Earlier

When Lisa was three years old, her father would put Pachelbel's *Canon in D* on the record player, hold on to both her hands, and spin her like a larriette. For the rest of her life, she loved classical music and any kind of dance. She was on the school dance team when she was in high school and, as an adult, her favorite film was the Shirley MacLaine / Anne Bancroft ballet film, *The Turning Point.* She understood the conflict in that story because the only thing Lisa wanted more than a chance to dance was a child.

Lisa and her husband, Mark, had been trying to get pregnant for over a year without success. Throughout her life a black cloud of sadness often engulfed her, and this failure brought in the thickest, darkest period of depression she had ever experienced.

One night Lisa lay on her back, crying.

Mark sat up in bed. He reached for her face, wiped the tears from her cheeks, then placed his hand on her shoulder, tugging her softly so she would face him. "We need to do something about this."

"What?" she asked, sniffling. Her voice grew louder. "We've been taking my temperature, timing my cycle, and fucking on schedule for over a year but still no results. I don't know what else we can do."

"That's not what I mean. I'm confident everything will work out if we keep trying but meanwhile, we need to help you handle this depression."

She shook her head. "I will not let some crazy psychiatrist put me on a drug that will leave me unable to feel anything. That's like being dead and God knows what it would do to our child if I do get pregnant."

"*When* you get pregnant," he said, quietly.

Lisa shrugged.

"I've got another idea, a better idea."

"I hope it's better than drugs."

"I want to take a ballroom dancing class with you. I found one."

"*You* want to take a dance class? You're stiff as a penguin."

Mark laughed. "Maybe so but you're graceful as a bird in flight and I want to be there to support you."

"No, Mark. The dance class is a good idea but I'll go by myself. The time alone will do me good."

He winced.

Lisa paused before asking, "Where is this class?"

"East Hanover."

It was a group class, organized by a women's club. A few of the women brought their husbands but, except for the instructor, those were the only men in the class. The class was taught by a medium-height man who had come to this country from Ukraine ten years earlier. He was now in his thirties and still spoke with an East European accent. He was dressed in all black except for a subtle gold pattern on the front of his shirt. His muscular legs showed through his stretch dance pants. The pants also emphasized another part of his anatomy. Lisa had to force herself not to stare.

His arms were covered with baggy sleeves but they were probably as fit as his legs. Lisa thought he was handsome with his dark hair, his short-cropped beard, as well as his very fit body.

The class began with the students lined up individually in three rows of ten. The instructor started the music, faced the group, and held his arms up. He was demonstrating good posture and how dancers should hold their shoulders to create the best lines. He moved on from there with a brief discussion of how to hold a partner.

Lisa was in the first line of the group and was a good dancer. When the instructor wanted everyone to try what he'd been discussing, he chose her as his partner. She glanced at her wedding ring, then politely turned him down. Lisa moved to the back of the group and partnered with a woman who was a rather awkward dancer. She wondered if she would have been better off with her penguin husband.

"You're so good," the woman told her during their break time.

"I've been dancing most of my life."

"It shows." She tilted her head before asking. "Then why did you take this class?"

"My husband thought it would get my mind off some things that are bothering me. By the way, my name is Lisa Thomas."

"Nice to meet you, Lisa. I'm Nancy, Nancy Walsh."

"And why did *you* take the class, Nancy?"

Nancy laughed. "I'm an actress but my roles are limited because I can't dance well. I thought this might help. I'm also a huge fan of Ginger Rogers."

Lisa leaned forward. "Ginger Rogers? Why didn't you pick someone current, somebody like—Janet Jackson?"

"It's a long story, but it comes down to something simple. A good friend gave me a pair of Ginger Rogers' shoes. I think she wore them in *Top Hat*. They're autographed. I've been a fan ever since."

Lisa's eyes went wide. "Really? The shoes she actually wore in the film?"

"Well…She wore more than one pair, I'm sure. But the ones I have look like the pair she had on when she and Fred Astaire were singing *Cheek to Cheek*."

"Wow! And that's why you took this class?"

"I can sing well enough and I'm a professional actress but I've never been a good dancer. I've got a nice sense of rhythm and I can move around my room to any song without missing a beat but I can't remember steps I've been taught. I've taken classes before without much success. I thought I'd try again."

"That's called muscle memory. You can develop it with practice."

"Maybe most people can but not me. There's another thing, too."

"What's that?"

"Like you, I've got a problem I want to forget."

Lisa's hand went to her mouth. "Really?"

Nancy shook her head. "Not exactly. I don't want to forget. What I really want is to find someone who will listen and not judge me."

Lisa smiled. "When the class is done, why don't you and I get something to eat? You can tell me your problem and I'll tell you mine. There are a couple of Italian places around the corner from here. We can go to one of those."

"That sounds nice."

Both women had brought clothes to wear over their leotards and tights. They slipped into those when the class was done, left Nancy's car in the parking lot of the dance hall, and drove Lisa's to a pizzeria. In just over ten minutes they were sitting across from each other, sipping cokes, eating pizza, and sharing their stories.

It didn't take the two women long to discover their problems were similar.

Lisa went first. When it was Nancy's turn she spoke in a soft, monotone. "Unlike you and Mark, my doctor knows what's wrong with me. My uterus doesn't function properly and they can't fix it. I've known this for a long time. I was even happy about it for a while since it meant I didn't have a period." She sat up straight. "No blood-stained white pants for me." She tried to laugh but her voice cracked.

"I lived with Scott for a few years without telling him but when he suggested we get married, I finally let him know. He said he loved me and wouldn't give me up for any reason. He suggested we adopt. I've thought about that, of course, and I know we'd be happy. Still, I feel guilty. Maybe it's because I waited to tell him until he loved me enough to ask me to marry him. Maybe it's because I'm the one with the physical problem. I don't know, but it bothers me."

Lisa reached across the table and took Nancy's hand. "You told him so you shouldn't feel guilty. A lot of women I know would never have mentioned a health issue like that. Scott told you he's fine with adoption so you need to take him at his word. We're also thinking of adopting but we're going to try a little longer. I've started meditating. I figure if stress is causing our problem then meditation will help solve it."

This new friendship was a wonderful thing for Nancy. It became even better when she learned Lisa lived just a block away from the lake, on the east shore. They began seeing more of each other. Since the weather was nice, they began meeting at Nancy's house on Halsey Island. The women planned to meet at Lisa's during the colder months.

Lisa always walked to the Windlass restaurant where Scott and Nancy would pick her up in Scott's Chris-Craft. Nancy knew Scott rode with her because he didn't want her driving his precious boat but she didn't complain.

"I believe Scott likes me spending time with you because I whine about infertility to you instead of him." Nancy intended that statement to be funny, but neither woman laughed.

"I think you're right," Lisa replied. "Mark acts the same way."

They were sitting in the wicker rockers on Nancy's porch, enjoying the warm, July night—sipping on gin and tonics, looking at the lake and the stars. There was only a tiny breeze and a few small clouds. The moon was just a sliver, which was nice because the limited light allowed Nancy to pick out Hercules, one of the few constellations she could recognize.

Lisa sat up straight and leaned forward. "I saw a shooting star. Is there supposed to be a meteor shower tonight?"

Nancy looked, following her friend's gaze. "I guess so." She paused. "I just saw one, too."

They both made wishes. Telling each other what they'd wished for would ruin the magic but Nancy knew Lisa had wished for the same thing she had—to have a baby.

A month and a half after that peaceful night, they were back together in Lisa's house. They'd chosen to meet on the mainland because it was a rainy September night. This way Lisa wouldn't have to get soaked while traveling from the mainland to the island. Nancy would still get wet but Nancy was used to this. She wore rain gear with pants and a hooded jacket.

After Nancy took off her rain apparel in Lisa's bathroom, she touched up her makeup and went out to sit with Lisa in the living room. Nancy thought Lisa might be expecting when she poured a glass of wine for Nancy but a Coke for herself. She said nothing because she didn't want to steal her friend's thunder.

Lisa's eyes sparkled. "You know those wishes we made in July?"

"When we were out on my porch?"

"Yes. Well…mine came true."

"You're pregnant?"

Lisa nodded.

When Lisa confirmed Nancy's hunch, a swarm of feelings stung her. There was jealousy because Lisa could have a child and she couldn't. There was anger because God had allowed her to be born with a damaged womb. There was self-hatred because she felt she was disappointing Scott. But there was also joy because a new life would come into the world and Nancy was certain her friend would allow her to help with the baby as much as she wanted to.

Nancy stood up, stepped to Lisa, and hugged her. When Nancy let go, Lisa was beaming.

"If it's a girl, I'm thinking of naming her Nancy."

Her entire body felt warm, but she shook her head. "I am so honored. It's just that it could be confusing. I was thinking your child might call me Aunt Nancy. She can't do that if we share the same name."

"We could call her Little Nancy and you Big Nancy."

"Cute. But please don't."

They both laughed.

"All right. I'll come up with another name. There's plenty of time."

"Do you know the due date?"

"April 2nd."

"Really? I hope she isn't born a day early. That would give her a birthday on April Fools' Day."

Lisa grinned. "Not the worst problem to be born with."

Nancy felt a pulse in her throat. Lisa's comment had been innocent enough, but it reminded Nancy of her own birth defect, her worthless womb. She needed to give some more thought to adopting.

Chapter Thirteen

Lisa did not want to use drugs during the birth so she and Mark took a Lamaze class to get ready. She planned to deal with the pain through the exercises the instructor taught them. Mark was her class partner. He wanted to be as much a part of the process as he could and loved learning what was happening inside Lisa's body. But he went to work every day.

Nancy didn't work. "I can come over as often as you want." Her words were rushed. "I can practice with you whenever you need me."

"That's nice. Can you come tomorrow morning?"

"Of course. Is eight o'clock OK?"

"Make it nine."

"Sure."

The pregnancy seemed easy compared to some of the horror stories Lisa had heard. She went through many of the common things women speak about: feeling nauseous (especially in the morning), craving strange foods (pickles wrapped in cheese), and constipation (Nancy offered to give her an enema but Lisa turned her down and did it herself). Lisa's ankles swelled, and she grew fat all over. She thought she was ugly, but Mark and Nancy assured her she was beautiful.

Her back started aching around the sixth month. Lisa's friend and her husband both offered her back rubs. Nancy's massages were wonderful but Mark's fingers were stronger and sometimes strayed into her pants, which Lisa liked—a lot.

Finally, the day came. Mark was at work, and Nancy was at her house when the contractions began. Lisa timed them the way the Lamaze instructor had taught her. When she was sure they were coming often enough and lasting long enough, she called Mark at work and Nancy at her winter home. Lisa asked Nancy to pick her up since she was the closest.

Nancy sat with Lisa until Mark arrived, then left the two of them in the labor room and moved to the waiting room. Lisa couldn't have asked for a better friend. She was in labor for less than eight hours, which seemed like an eternity to Lisa but was much less than average for the birth of a first child. Lisa wanted to let Nancy know when the staff moved her to the delivery room but there was no way she could do that.

The Lamaze exercises worked perfectly and there were no complications. Cassie was born, cleaned up, and resting on Lisa's chest in less than an hour from when Lisa was fully dilated.

After Lisa moved to the recovery room, she asked Mark to find Nancy so he could tell her how things had gone.

* * *

Lisa seemed happy to share her child with Nancy, who would come to visit and hold her new daughter. Nancy would babysit for them once a week so they could go out to dinner. She loved Cassie and loved Lisa for being so welcoming. But things were not working as well between Nancy and Scott.

The talk of adoption dwindled after Cassie was born as did their sex life. Nancy was at Lisa's home often which limited their time together and lessened how close they felt to each other. And when they made love, there was sadness over them, like a thick shroud. Nancy didn't understand why they felt that way but later she came to think the sorrow was a foreshadowing of the dark event to come.

It was a Friday morning. Nancy was scheduled to babysit that night. The plan was for her to visit Lisa in the afternoon, chat for a while, then share the cuddling and feeding of Cassie and the changing of her diapers. This was their normal routine for days when Nancy was to babysit.

She overslept that morning and didn't get up until 8:30. All she had planned to do before leaving for Lisa's, was some vacuuming and dusting so she had plenty of time. Nancy normally fixed Scott's breakfast, but he already had the coffee on and had eaten a bowl of cereal when she came into the kitchen, still in her nightgown. She felt bad about that but he was fine with it. He even told her she looked good, which she was sure was a lie. She hadn't combed her hair and her nightgown was old, with a couple of rips in the material.

After Scott walked out the back door, Nancy poured coffee for herself, stuck a slice of bread in the toaster, then fried an egg and a couple of strips of bacon. She felt guilty that Scott had a skimpy breakfast while she was treating herself to a feast, but it had been his choice. He could have woken her.

She had only swallowed two forkfuls of egg, and toast before the phone rang. She wondered who would call her at that time. When she picked up the receiver there was a brief silence before she heard what she thought was Lisa's voice. There were no words and the sounds Nancy heard were shaky and soft.

"What's wrong?" Nancy asked.

"It's…it's…oh…oh." Lisa's voice faded.

"Tell me! Are you okay?"

"It's…it's Cassie."

"What's happened to her? Is Mark there?"

"No. He's gone."

"Gone? Did he leave you?"

"No. Of course not. He went to work."

"What about Cassie? What happened?"

"I went to wake her." Lisa was crying, barely getting the words out. "She was so still. I thought she was sleeping but when I turned her to her back, I could see her belly wasn't moving."

Nancy could hear Lisa struggle to take in a breath then there was silence.

"Tell me!" Nancy shouted.

"She's dead!"

"Oh, my God! Did you call the hospital?"

"I called you first."

"Okay. Hang up. Then dial 911 and get somebody to help you. Maybe there's something that can be done. Meanwhile, I'll get dressed and be over there as soon as I can. Oh, Lisa. This is horrible!"

Chapter Fourteen

2022

Silence engulfed the room as Lisa's voice fell quiet. Susie didn't know what to say and, judging by the way Kyle and Taylor looked, they didn't either.

"And that was it." Lisa finally spoke in a thick, low voice. "The ambulance arrived and took Cassie away. I didn't go with them. They said I could but I couldn't get out of the chair I was in. I couldn't walk. I needed to wait for your mother. I needed someone to hug me and tell me what happened wasn't my fault." Lisa sighed so long Susie wondered if she was trying to suffocate. "It didn't go that way, not exactly. Your mother wouldn't touch me and between her sobs, she asked if I'd put Cassie to sleep on her stomach. I nodded because I had." Her voice broke. "I could see Nancy knew I caused Cassie's death. I could see it in her eyes." Lisa looked down at her feet. "She drove me to the hospital. They had Cassie in a room so at least she wasn't in the morgue. That was the last time I saw my daughter. Mark handled everything from that point on. He had her cremated and picked up her ashes when that was done. He scattered them somewhere in the lake. I don't know where and I never want to know. Cassie is gone. That's all that matters. And now you tell me Nancy has died, too. But for me, your mother was gone a long time ago. She stopped coming by my house, calling me, or even talking to me when I called her. My marriage to Mark lasted just long enough for him to file for divorce. I don't speak to him anymore. I do not know if he's alive or dead." Lisa paused again, then looked at Susie. "Life is Hell. You're born, you suffer, and you die. That's it."

Kyle, Taylor, and Susie left Lisa's house in silence. When they were in the car, about to pull out of the driveway, Susie leaned forward and clutched Kyle and Taylor's seats. "Oh, my God," she said, her voice shaking like a train off its tracks.

Kyle shook his head. "Yes. What a sad person."

Susie could feel her heart beating fast and strong. "This is not about her."

"It's not?" Kyle asked.

Susie wrung her hands and brought them to her mouth. "My Mom couldn't have children. Now I know for certain. I was adopted and no one ever told me."

Taylor turned back to look at Susie, her eyes wide. "That's what this search is about! Your mom wanted you to know the secret of your life!"

"Yes. She wants me to find my birth parents."

* * *

Susie was on edge when she returned to her apartment.

She called Danny. "I want to see you tonight. Can I buy you dinner?"

"Of course."

"You up for Italian?"

"At Frank's?"

"Yes. I can pick you up at 5:00."

"Sounds good."

She was still feeling tense as they sat in the restaurant. She had dressed in an outfit Danny liked—a sheer pink blouse and a flared, gray skirt. Under those, she wore white lace panties and a matching demi bra. Her shoes were black pumps with two-inch heels.

She wanted to tell him what she'd learned about her mother but couldn't seem to get the words out, even after he asked her how the meeting with Lisa had gone. She was furious with her parents. They had lied to her for her entire life and she couldn't understand why. Maybe it was a generation thing. Nowadays, adopting is something to be proud of but years ago that might not have been the case.

Danny swallowed the last bite of his chicken marsala. "What did she say about the missing shoe?"

"Not much," Susie told him. "She said Mom mentioned them once and told her a friend gave them to her but that's all she remembered."

"So a wasted trip?"

"Not exactly. Why don't we ask for a couple of cannolis in a takeout box and head over to my place? I've got a nice red zinfandel I'd like to share with you."

Danny smiled and nodded.

When they reached her apartment building, they climbed the stairs to her second-floor room. She pulled out a couple of glasses and the wine but before she opened the bottle she said, "Can we go to the bedroom first? I need you to hold me."

"Was what Lisa said that bad?"

"I'll tell you later but I need you now." She took his hand and led him to her bed.

Although their sex life had always been good, that evening was intense. Danny was generally the initiator and almost always gentle. This time Susie took the lead. They usually took off their clothes before climbing under the covers. Instead, Susie pulled Danny to her and kissed him, pushing her lips against his as hard as she ever had. Only then did they fall to the bed together, on top of the bedspread. That's when they undressed each other, throwing their clothes all over the room. Danny was naked and Susie had lost her top and her underwear, but still had her skirt on, pushed up around her waist. It had buttons that would take too much time and neither of them could wait any longer. Danny started on top but Susie made him roll over so she would have control. She kissed him on his lips, his neck, his chest, and all the way down his body. He tried to return the kisses but she wouldn't let him. She needed this.

When the sex was over Danny was panting. "That was…"

"Desperate?"

"I was going to say amazing."

They were side by side on the bed. The bedspread and covers had all been kicked off. They were naked except for the gray skirt Susie still wore around her waist like a belt. Susie was staring at the ceiling, trying to figure out where all that energy had come from. Was it from her attraction to Kyle? Was it from her frustration with how little she'd learned about Ginger's other shoe? Was it from her anger with her parents hiding her birth history? All she knew for sure was it had nothing to do with Danny and she was ashamed of that.

"Let's get dressed and open the wine."

Danny shook his head slowly. "Can we stay here a little longer? This is Heaven."

"You can if you like but I need a drink," she told him, still not looking into his eyes.

"OK. I'll come."

It took them a minute to find their clothes and dress. They started to make the bed but Susie noticed a wet spot. She pulled the sheets off, crumpled them up, and tossed them on the floor. "I'll take care of this later."

The zinfandel was Bedrock Old Vine. It was the first time in years she'd spent over twenty dollars on a standard-size bottle of wine. She could have opened a nine-dollar bottle of the Australian brand. Danny wouldn't have known the difference but Susie had a need for the good stuff.

They sat across from each other at the table in her great room. She poured their drinks, swallowing a mouthful of hers without taking time to appreciate the taste. It was time to tell Danny what she'd learned. "I was adopted."

"Really? That's interesting."

"Yes, it is. It's also something I just learned today."

Danny's eyes narrowed. "You're kidding. Why would your parents keep that from you?"

"All I know is two things. My mother couldn't have children, which is what I learned today from Lisa, and my birth certificate lists the people I've been calling Mom and Dad as my actual parents."

"That's odd. Could Lisa have been wrong?"

Susie clenched her hands. "I don't think so. She sounded sincere while she told us a very long and personal story. She claimed Mom was her close friend and helped Lisa take care of her baby until the child died of infant death syndrome. It sounded as if Mom got very possessive about that little girl but Lisa claimed she wasn't jealous. She appreciated the help. Why would Lisa go through all of that just to tell a lie?"

"I see your point."

Susie pursed her lips and whispered. "It would explain my eye color. My parents both had brown eyes. I always assumed they had recessive genes."

"Both of them? Not likely."

"Exactly."

"Still, if your parents weren't your birth parents then how did the certificate get changed?"

She shook her head. "Maybe they knew somebody who could get that done."

Danny wanted to stay overnight but Susie said no so he headed home.

Chapter Fifteen

The next evening Taylor called.

"I've been thinking about the things Lisa told us." Taylor's voice grew softer. "This is getting interesting."

"I don't think *interesting* is the right word," Susie replied, shaking her head at the phone. "My parents lied to me and I want to know why."

"I understand but I think we need to approach this in a different direction." She paused. "I said that wrong. We still need to talk to Theresa Robinson but while we're waiting to go to her home, I would like to research your mother. Maybe I can find out why she would not be honest with you. Or I might find something that shows Lisa was wrong. Either way, it will help us learn more about her."

"Research?"

"There's a theater library in Lincoln Center where they keep hundreds of original programs and director's notes from New York productions. I want to go there and look through whatever is available. There could be something in their records that might give us a clue. You told me your mom was an actress for a while, right?"

"Yes. Before I was born."

"Then they might have something about her. Also, I can look into the registrar in the town that issued your birth certificate. Maybe they've had a history of not following the rules."

"Oh, Taylor. That's wonderful!"

"Do you know any of the plays she was in? In particular, ones that were big enough to keep records."

"The only one I can remember was called *Last Summer at Bluefish Cove*. She was in an off-broadway production."

"Really? I know that play. It was an important show. It was one of the first plays to present lesbian characters that weren't stereotypes. Could your mom have been gay? It was harder to come out back then."

She shook her head. "There was no way Mom was like that. My dad and mom had a good relationship."

"Maybe you're right. I shouldn't confuse the actress with the character she played but it might have been easier to get the part if she had the same orientation as the other women working on the show."

"Easier how?" Susie's voice was tight.

"Forget I said that."

Susie was breathing harder. "I'm sure my mother did not like girls in that way and I know she would not have cheated on my dad for a part in a play—any play. So don't go there."

There was an uncomfortable pause in the conversation after Susie's reaction and a short time later Taylor hung up. Susie was worried she might have hurt Taylor's feelings, but she was defending her mother's honor. She knew her mother well enough to know what she was suggesting couldn't be true. That's what she told herself but Taylor's words kept ringing in her head and she wondered if she was being defensive.

* * *

The following night Taylor came by her apartment. Susie had planned to catch up on some reading. She changed into her nightgown early, a white, cotton gown decorated with holly leaves and berries. She settled into her favorite reading chair with the Susan Wiggs' romance novel she'd started a week earlier and was surprised when Taylor arrived. "I didn't know you were coming over."

"I took time off from work and went to New York. I had some success at the library today and wanted to let you know."

"All right" She opened the door and let her in.

"I looked through the director's notes for *Last Summer at Bluefish Cove* and found nothing interesting but I discovered Nancy had the female lead in a play called *Romantic Comedy*. It was at the Paper Mill Playhouse in Millburn and you'll never guess who was the male lead."

Taylor paused long enough for Susie to say, "Please don't make me guess."

"All right. It was Phil Robinson, the husband of Nancy's friend Theresa."

"Phil Robinson was an actor?"

"He was a politician. They're all actors."

"But you're saying he was a professional actor? Is that right?"

"He and your mom were co-leads in that play."

"This is good, Taylor. It gives me something other than the shoe to ask about when we drop in on her. Theresa was my mother's friend but maybe Mom was close to Phil as well."

"Do you think they could have had an affair?"

"Why would you think that?"

Taylor leaned toward her. "I didn't find a pattern of mishandling documents in the Morris County Vital Records department. But somebody changed your birth certificate and Phil Robinson might have been able to do that. He was involved in politics." She swallowed before continuing with a firm voice. "There's another possibility here and you should be prepared."

"What's that?"

"If your parents had your birth certificate changed, they might have done other illegal things."

"Such as?"

"It's possible you weren't adopted. You might have been kidnapped."

Susie felt as if someone had punched her in the throat. "Kidnapped?"

Taylor put her palms together and brought them to her lips. "More people do it than you think, people who are desperate for a child. I was reading an article about missing babies just the other day."

Susie clenched her jaw. "You're being ridiculous. First, you tell me she was gay and traded her body for a role, then you say she was having an affair with the husband of one of her best friends, and now you say she was involved with stealing babies! Listen. I was young when my father died but I knew my parents well. They had a great relationship. When my father died, my mother was devastated. We both were, but she picked herself up and continued to be an example to me. She was kind, loving, and honest. She wouldn't have cheated on my dad with anyone, male or female. And she certainly wouldn't have been involved with kidnapping a baby. There has to be another explanation."

* * *

The next day Taylor's assumptions still confused and angered Susie. Taylor was nice for helping her look for the missing shoe but those accusations were plain crazy. Her mother would not have done any of those things.

Susie thought of how Kyle would never have had a mean word to say about her mother. Unlike Taylor, he and Susie had a connection from their childhood days that could never break. They were destined to be together. She wished Taylor would just go away.

Susie's thoughts and emotions were confusing, from her feelings toward Kyle to the unanswered questions brought out by her mother's last request. Susie hated when her life was so messy. That's one reason she loved acting. On stage, her lines were written for her and her emotions were clear. It didn't matter if the words filled her with hate or love as long as she knew what she was supposed to feel. Real life was different, and it irritated her.

Chapter Sixteen

There was another box in the closet where Taylor had found the single shoe. It contained old tax forms, copies of what Susie's parents had filed decades earlier. She wondered why they'd left them in the house after Kyle's grandfather bought it. The simplest answer was they must have forgotten the box was there. Taylor knew how important financial records were but some people didn't think the way she did.

The papers were old enough to shred, but she thought destroying them should be Susie's decision. Taylor hadn't mentioned her discovery to Susie, because she wanted to go through them before she turned them over. She started reading them the day after her visit with Susie. Kyle was home but working outside that day, replacing a couple of cleats on his sailboat and cleaning the boathouse walls.

Taylor loved old tax returns. They revealed so much about people's priorities. The first thing she looked for was the child deduction. She found they took it in their 1998 joint form. Susie was the same age as Kyle so she was a newborn that year. Susie would have no recollection of any parents other than Nancy and Scott.

There were records for the next twelve years. Taylor found nothing interesting. They kept listing Susie as a dependent, of course. Also, Nancy started creating and selling jewelry in 2000. She operated that small craft business at a loss for two years, then gave up listing it.

After going through the records from the years following Susie's arrival, Taylor switched to the preceding years. Nancy had some income from acting from 1978 to 1997 but there was nothing after that. It was clear Susie's arrival had stopped Nancy's career. At that point, she discovered something unusual and interesting. Nancy and Scott had given Theresa Robinson's husband, Phil, a gift of $7,000 in 1997, a massive gift for their modest income. It seemed to Taylor they must have received something in return. But what?

Taylor put the papers back in the box and headed out to speak to Kyle. She wanted to get his opinion before she called Susie.

"Tax records?" Kyle tilted his head. "Why did you wait so long to say anything?"

"Susie's busy with this search, I thought I'd wait until I went through them all but what I discovered may be important."

He narrowed his eyes. "I understand your thinking but you should have told me."

"You would have insisted I tell Susie. You're too close to her."

"I suppose that's right." He chuckled. "Still, you need to tell her now."

"Do you want to be on the phone with me?"

"Just let me know what she says." He turned back to washing the boathouse wall.

Taylor went to the main house and up to the lakeside bedroom where she had left the box of tax returns. She called Susie from there so she could look at the paperwork if she needed to answer questions.

The phone rang. Susie saw the name on the screen, took in a deep breath, and picked it up. "Kyle?"

"It's me, Taylor." That wasn't the voice she was expecting.

Susie sighed. "What do you want?" Taylor's accusations about her mother still irritated her.

"There's something else I need to discuss with you," Taylor said.

"Oh?" Susie cleared her throat. "This isn't about my relationship with Kyle, is it?"

There was a pause before Taylor said, "It isn't."

"Well…Before you say anything. I want you to know I've got a boyfriend and I don't intend to leave him."

"That's interesting."

"Kyle and I were very close when we were young. That's all there is to it. I know I worry you and I want to clear the air. There is *nothing* between us."

"That's nice."

"Yes, it is. No conflict there, believe me."

"I'm glad you aren't interested. It makes things simpler."

"I didn't say I wasn't interested. I said I have a boyfriend."

"Whatever. It was wonderful talking to you. I'm going to hang up now." And that's what she did. Susie heard the sarcasm in Taylor's tone and that irritated her even more.

"Call her back." Taylor turned to see Kyle in the doorway, his arms crossed. His nostrils were flaring. The only other time she'd seen him with an expression like that was when someone in a speedboat almost rammed them. And back then he wasn't angry with *her*.

"You should have heard her. I called to help. You know that. All she wanted to say was that you and she have a connection but she will not leave her boyfriend. Is that true? About the connection?"

"Of course it is. I've known her since we were children. You can't just erase years of friendship overnight. But you and I have something we've formed as adults. You said she doesn't want to leave her boyfriend. Well, I don't want to leave you."

"Then tell me that."

"I just did."

"Not until after you ordered me to call her back!" She could feel sweat forming on her arms and chest. "You don't even talk to the people who work for you like that!"

"Calm down, Taylor." He put his hands on her shoulders, looked into her eyes, and took a deep breath. He was showing her how to get control but she didn't want to lose the anger she felt. She stepped away and turned her back toward him. Kyle kept talking in a calm tone. "This isn't about *me* and Susie and it isn't about *you* and Susie. It's about *us* and her. We've committed to helping her solve this problem, and that's what we need to do. If you don't call her back and explain about the tax records, then I will."

Taylor understood what Kyle was saying. This time she followed his lead and breathed deeply before saying, "All right. I'll call."

The phone rang again. Susie saw Kyle's name on the screen and knew it was Taylor calling back. She picked it up and said, "I'm sorry, Taylor. I was in a bad mood and I took it out on you. It had nothing to do with you or with Kyle. Actually, I appreciate you spending a vacation day in the library researching my mom. I didn't like everything you said, but it's all helpful."

"You and I are OK."

"No, we're not. What I mean is you shouldn't be OK with me. You couldn't have expected me to come barreling back into Kyle's life but you reacted by helping me with my crazy search. I value that. Really. I do."

"Your search isn't crazy. That's what I was calling about. It's…uh…something else," Taylor seemed to struggle to find the right word. "…essential. You are learning about your history and I need to tell you this."

"What?" Susie sat and switched her phone to her other ear.

"I found tax records."

"I don't understand."

"They're old forms your parents filed from before you were born and some years after."

"Really?"

"Yes. I found them in a box next to the one with the single shoe. I didn't want to bother you unless I found something important, so I went through them."

"And you found something?"

"That's right. Your parents gave Phil Robinson a gift of $7,000 in 1997."

"The year before I was born?"

"Uh huh."

"Oh God. You were right. That's why I was in such a bad mood. I was worried you might have been right and now it seems you were. They probably kidnapped me when I was an infant."

"You think the money was to pay someone to steal you for your parents?"

"It makes sense. What do *you* think?"

"I think we need to talk to Phil Robinson next. I've located him and his wife. They still live near the lake."

Taylor volunteered to reach out to them to set a date but Susie wanted to surprise them. "The way we did with Lisa Thomas. That worked well."

Taylor's voice dropped to a lower pitch. "They may not be ready to entertain unexpected visitors."

"They don't need to entertain us."

"No, they don't. But they'll think they do if we drop by without calling first."

"None of that matters. If they're a little uncomfortable, they may talk more."

"I suppose you're right." Taylor tightened her grip on the phone. "Can you spend another night at our house? That would give us an entire day to enjoy the lake and talk before heading over there."

Susie remembered the noisy sex she'd heard the last time and intended to deal with that issue. "I'd like to bring Danny if that's all right."

"That's fine."

"One thing," Susie said.

"What's that?"

Susie smiled at the phone. "I'll do the cooking."

"You want to do that?"

"Yes. I'll bring everything I need and I remember that kitchen well. It will be fun."

Chapter Seventeen

Taylor wore her cut-off jeans and a blue tank top with no bra. Kyle could see the outline of her nipples through the thin material as he watched her climb into the Chris-Craft. *Susie, be damned,* he thought. But that thought disappeared as soon as they reached the Bridge Marina where Susie and Danny were waiting.

Kyle had missed Susie for his entire adult life. They were just kids when they had been best friends but he'd always thought about her. He'd tried to imagine what she was up to and to picture the woman she'd grown into. When she showed up at his work party, he found her more beautiful than those musings had led him to believe. Feelings emerged he had trouble suppressing. When Kyle heard Susie was to spend another night on the island, he knew he'd have to be careful. He didn't want to mess up what he had with Taylor. It was good Taylor would be with them the whole time and even better that Susie had invited Danny. But he would still have to be careful or he might trigger a reaction from Taylor he'd have trouble reversing.

They were by the gas pumps at the end of the marina's dock. Susie was wearing black shorts and a matching, loose t-shirt with a scoop neck. She got down on her knees when they pulled up and lowered her bag to the boat floor. Kyle could see down her shirt to the drawstring on her shorts, right over the black bikini top she was wearing underneath. Or was it a bra? He wasn't sure. Susie's breasts weren't as large as Taylor's. Still, he liked everything about the way she looked.

Susie held her neckline as she stood. She'd most likely noticed where his gaze had been. This was not a good way to start the evening.

When they reached the house, Susie went straight from the boat to the kitchen to prepare the meal she'd brought.

She served a spinach quiche along with fruit salad and hash browns. The meal was simple but delicious. The women drank Vermentino Sauvignon Blanc while Danny and Kyle drank Cape May white ale.

Kyle and Susie did most of the talking, reminiscing about their adventures when they were children. They told a story of skimming buttons in a strange way. It was Kyle's idea. They replaced the lure on a fishing line with a shank button so they could skim it and reel it back in. Kyle won the skimming contests but Susie had one great cast and held the record—12 skips. Taylor and Danny smiled and laughed but didn't talk as much as the other two.

They all seemed to relax by the time Susie brought the desert out. She had bought chocolate cupcakes, one for each and two extra to either split or fight over. The coffee she served did little to diminish the buzz Kyle was feeling, and it appeared the others were in the same state. This was when they began discussing the shoe Susie wanted to find.

Everyone was talking at once until Taylor pushed her chair back, stood, and slowly waved her arm around the table in a gesture meant to silence the other conversations. "We know about the $7,000 gift in 1997." Her voice was slurring slightly, but she took a breath and controlled it. She started again. "It's time to talk about the relationship between Phil Robinson and Nancy Walsh." Her voice was clearer, but she was speaking slowly and enunciating each word carefully. Kyle was glad he wasn't the only one who had drunk a little too much.

Susie pressed her lips together. "You think there was a relationship?" She paused for a moment then continued in a softer voice. "I still think you're wrong. I didn't see that when I was young." Her words were clear. Perhaps she'd had less wine than Kyle thought she had.

"I think it's possible. They were in that production of *Romantic Comedy* in 1993, five years before you were born. Nancy might have been an entirely different person back then."

"She married my dad in 1991."

"I believe she met Phil on the set of that play which is a story about a married man falling in love with someone other than his wife. Whether or not your mother had an affair doesn't make any difference. They must have grown close and four years later she gave him a huge cash gift. Something suspicious was going on there."

Susie's eyes narrowed. "I've been in plenty of plays and never once slept with a co-star."

Taylor shook her head. "We'll ask Phil about the play when we talk to him tomorrow. If an opportunity to bring up the money arises, we can ask about that, but regardless we can ask about the play. It's innocent enough."

After dinner, Taylor and Susie cleaned up the dishes while Kyle and Danny went out on the porch to talk and finish their coffees.

Susie rubbed the back of her neck as she stared at the dishes in the sink.

"I'll do them if you like," Taylor said, chuckling. "The dishes and silverware are all mine, anyway. Your cake pan is in the refrigerator with a couple of slices of quiche still in it and your other two bowls won't take me but a minute."

"That's not the point. The guys are relaxing while we're in here cleaning up. That isn't fair. I did the cooking."

"Don't worry about it. This gives us a chance to talk."

"Oh no." Susie bit her lip. "Is this about the way I acted on the phone? I've already apologized. You caught me in a horrible mood."

"It's not that. I want to get to know you better." Taylor put her hands on Susie's shoulders and steered her to one of the kitchen chairs. "You sit here and we can talk while I finish these dishes."

"You shouldn't have to do that."

"It's fine. I'm just going to rinse them and put them in the dishwasher. Meanwhile, I'd like to hear more about you. I want to know why you're the only childhood friend Kyle ever mentions."

"All right but you go first. I know nothing about your life before Kyle."

"OK." Taylor put a plate in the dishwasher. She turned to Susie and leaned back against the counter. She put her palms together to form a steeple with her fingers, then pressed her hands against her lips.

"I love Kyle." Taylor paused to see if Susie reacted. When Susie didn't flinch, she continued. "My life before him was nice but often lonely."

"Weren't there other men?"

"At times. But nothing serious. I was after something more, something that would last a long time. The only relationship that ever came close to what I wanted was in college with another accounting major. Her name was Camilla. We were best friends until she let me know she wanted something more. I liked her. I can even say I loved her. But I was straight back then, and she was not. It was a confusing time for me. She didn't talk to me often after things between us got awkward and she transferred out of Fairleigh Dickinson at the end of that year."

Susie opened her mouth to say something but nothing came out.

Taylor smiled, then asked. "Did you ever kiss Kyle?"

Susie nodded. "We kissed twice when we were eight. We were playing Narnia. He was Caspian, and I was Susan. Like you and Camilla, things between us were awkward, but we got over it. Maybe because we were just kids. Anyway, we remained friends until I had to move away."

"That's not quite the same but thank you for telling me. Maybe that's why he never stopped thinking about you."

"We were friends. That's all. Now we're old friends who have some catching up to do but nothing else."

"So you said. You have Danny."

"I do." Susie looked down at her feet. She was wearing her sketchers with no socks.

Taylor took in a deep breath and let it out slowly. She tilted her head and looked at Susie, who was still sitting. She furrowed her brow, then asked, "Did you ever kiss a woman?"

Susie stood. She pushed her hair behind her ears and took a step back, away from Taylor. "Why do you ask?"

Taylor stepped toward Susie. "It's different."

"From kissing a man?"

"Yes, and certainly not the same as two eight-year-old kids imitating a scene from a Disney film."

"I get your point and to answer your question—I've never kissed a woman."

Susie moved to the sink and started washing the few dishes that were still waiting. When she was young, they washed everything by hand. Now there was an under-counter dishwasher replacing a cabinet that had been there, about the only change Kyle had made to the kitchen. The old stove was the same as was the refrigerator. The position of the sink was also the same as it had been. She pictured Taylor staring out the window, thinking while scrubbing pots and pans. She wondered what those thoughts would be.

Taylor moved next to Susie and gave her a small, soft hip bump to push her aside. "I'll finish these."

"If that's what you want."

"It is. You go out and talk to Kyle and Danny."

There was something going on in Taylor's head. She wasn't sure what it was but if a man was asking personal questions and touching her the way Taylor had, Susie would think he was interested.

Her thoughts went to Kyle. They were just restarting their friendship, but she still felt close to him. Taylor was his live-in partner. This confused Susie. If one of her female friends had a partner who asked personal questions about kissing, Susie would tell him to back off. At least, she *thought* she would.

So what should she do here? Taylor not only helped with the search for Ginger's shoe but she was eager to keep helping. She was kind but maybe a little too kind. Taylor said she told her college friend she was straight but then added that she'd been confused. She didn't sound confused anymore.

Susie was straight. That was certain. She'd thought about women with women but had never imagined herself in a relationship like that. All her fantasies were about men and she'd had lots of those. Yet she wanted to respect Taylor's right to whatever sexual preference she had. How should she react to this situation? And what about Kyle's feelings?

Susie dried her hands on the dish towel before she headed to the porch.

That night, as Susie lay in bed, she heard Kyle and Taylor making love again. She reached over and touched Danny's arm. He was awake and turned to her so they could kiss. As they made love her thoughts danced from Danny to Kyle to Danny to Kyle and every so often she imagined Taylor standing beside the bed, watching.

It was Susie's turn to feel confused.

Chapter Eighteen

Taylor served a wonderful breakfast on the porch: scrambled eggs, bacon, and English muffins. After they were done eating they stayed in their seats, sipping coffee and watching a half dozen sailboats on the lake.

It's not an official race," Kyle said. "Not enough of them."

Danny grinned. "Sailing looks fun."

"It seems peaceful," Susie agreed, "but you get in one of those boats and it's a lot of work. Still fun—in a different way."

"We can join them if you'd like," Kyle told Danny.

"Not until you two clear the table and do the dishes," Taylor said. "It's your turn."

The men didn't argue.

Taylor poured another cup of coffee for each of them. This was Susie's third which was about a normal morning's worth of caffeine for her. By the time she had drained her cup, the men were back. Danny and Kyle were in swimsuits and t-shirts. It had been a chilly morning but it was getting warmer quickly. They announced they were going sailing, then headed toward the water. As they started down the hill, Susie and Taylor stripped to the swimsuits they both wore under their sweatshirts and shorts, then followed.

The men went into the boathouse to rig the sailboat while the women went to a couple of chaise lounges on the dock where they could soak up the sun's rays. Taylor had on the same blue bikini she'd worn the day Susie first met her. This time Susie would not be outdone. She had on a black bikini that was almost as tiny as Taylor's. They were both wearing sunglasses. Susie needed hers to protect her sensitive eyes but Taylor also needed a pair since the sun was so bright.

Susie's skin was a lighter tone than Taylor's but they both used sunscreen. Taylor had the kind you spray on. They helped each other with their backs, then settled into the chairs to feel the warmth. After a minute or two of silence, Susie was the first to speak. "I was wondering if working at the same company as Kyle is difficult?"

"What do you mean?"

"Your relationship must be different at work than it is when you're at home."

"Well…" Taylor laughed. "There are some things we can do here that are not allowed in the office."

Susie grinned, then shook her head. "That's not what I mean. He's a higher level than you, isn't he?"

"Yeah, but it's not like he's my boss. Actually, we don't see each other that much at work. When we first were a couple, we would eat lunch together but projects would run into our lunch hours. It was a problem for both of us. I'm the one who suggested we stop that routine. One meal a day with Kyle was enough for me and I wanted to get to know the other people in my department better." She leaned back in the lounge chair and looked up at the sky. "It's your turn."

Susie's heart skipped. "My turn?"

"Tell me something about you and Kyle when you were children. I want to know what you were like, both of you."

She thought for a moment before speaking. "There was a time in kindergarten…"

"You were friends way back then?"

"Yeah. We were. Anyway, the class was making turkeys from handprints. You've seen those, haven't you?"

Taylor nodded.

"We had to get our entire hands filled with finger paints, then place them flat on the paper our teacher gave us. Only thing was Kyle wanted to put his handprint on top of mine. We ended up with this big glob with seven tail feathers instead of the normal four. His pointer finger covered my pinkie and his thumb wasn't visible, but other than that all our fingers made clear prints. The teacher loved it. She called it big mama turkey and put it in the center of the bulletin board."

"Is that when you first became friends?"

"No. We were in preschool together. I think our moms used to swap babysitting nights when we were infants."

"Wow. From birth, huh?"

"I believe so."

Susie leaned back on the lounge until she was horizontal with Taylor and told another kindergarten story. She was staring at the clouds as this second tale began but about halfway through she looked at Taylor and noticed she appeared to be asleep. Taylor's sunglasses covered her eyes so Susie couldn't tell if she'd shut them, but she was still and her breathing was even.

So much for my enthralling stories, Susie thought.

Taylor's stomach was smooth and moving gently. Susie studied her midsection from her ribcage to the bikini gap between her abdomen and the waistband of her suit bottoms. She watched as Taylor's flesh swelled with each intake of air, then came back down as she exhaled. Her skin was tan and blemish free. Only her belly button broke the flat surface, a lone whirlpool on a calm pond.

Taylor's breaths seemed to match the rhythm of the small waves breaking against the dock and the seawall. That vision, those sounds, and the smell of the freshwater gave Susie a feeling of euphoria. The day was absolutely beautiful.

Susie turned her head back to the sky and the soft, white clouds. She couldn't look at a woman the way Taylor did. She was drawn to solid strength rather than flexible strength—oak, not willow.

Susie closed her eyes and tried to sleep. If Taylor could drift off, so could she. She focused on the sound of the waves and the leaves rustling on the island shore. But before she could doze off, she felt something on her thigh. She opened her eyes. Taylor's hand was resting there, palm down. She turned to see if Taylor was still sleeping and it appeared she was. Perhaps she was pretending? If not, Susie didn't want to wake her.

Susie didn't think she'd drifted off but when she opened her eyes Taylor was gone. She looked out at the lake to see if the men were still sailing but didn't know one sail from another. She poked her head in the boathouse. The Thistle wasn't there, confirming her suspicion that Kyle's boat was one of the ones she saw. The men would probably be out on the water for most of the morning.

Susie hadn't burned thanks to the sunblock, but she was hot and sweaty. She took a quick dip before she went to the house to help Taylor prepare the lunch. The visit with Phil and Theresa Robinson would have to wait until after the men returned, the meal was done, and everyone had changed their clothes.

* * *

When the foursome finally made it to the Robinson's, Susie knocked on the door. A woman answered. She was short, no more than five foot two, with thick, white hair, penciled-in eyebrows, and an oval face. Except for the deep shade of her red lipstick, she could have passed for Paula Deen.

Taylor, Kyle, and Danny were standing behind Susie. The women were wearing button-up blouses while the men were even more casual in t-shirts. Danny's was a Rutgers t while Kyle's was solid black. All four wore blue jeans.

"May I help you?"

"Theresa?"

"Yes."

"I'm Susie Walsh, Nancy Walsh's daughter."

Theresa smiled, and her eyes sparkled. "How nice. It's been a long time since I've heard from her. How is she?"

"I'm sorry to have to tell you, but she passed." Susie decided not to tell her how recently this had happened.

"Oh, dear. I thought of her many times over the years. I wish I'd called her and now it's too late. Is there anything I can do for you?"

"Yes, there is. That's why I'm here. May we come in?"

"I'm afraid my husband isn't feeling well."

"Let her in." The man's voice from inside was weak and hoarse. "I want to talk to her."

"There are four people. I don't want you straining yourself."

"The rest of us can wait out here," Taylor said.

"No." The man coughed. "Tell them all to come in. I want to talk to Susie and her friends."

Theresa stepped back and opened the door wide. Susie entered and waited while Taylor, Kyle, and Danny climbed the front steps and followed. The house's first floor was a large open area with living room furniture in one section, dining room furniture in another, a kitchen off to the right, and what looked like a den in the back. There were posts holding up the upper floors instead of structural walls. A person in any place in that room could look through the front windows and the ones in the back without taking a single step. The lake was the scene in front, although the house had no waterfront. It was set back from the water but up a hill where the homes in front didn't block the view. The Robinson's home impressed Susie. These people had money.

The voice called again. "Come here. I want to see you."

Theresa walked toward the living room area where her husband was sitting in front of a television that was turned off. The others followed.

As they drew close to Phil, Susie noticed about a dozen pill containers on a snack table next to his recliner. *Theresa wasn't lying about him not feeling well. He was on serious meds.*

Phil didn't get up, but he turned his head to look at Susie. "We saw you some years back."

"You did?"

"Theresa and I saw you as Lily in *The Secret Garden*. You have a beautiful voice."

Susie relaxed. She looked up from the pills and into Phil's eyes. "Thank you. That show was a wonderful experience. I was eighteen playing the ghost of a woman about fifteen years older. It was a challenge."

"I'm glad you inherited Nancy's love of theater. I was an actor when I was younger."

"I know. You were in *Romantic Comedy* with my mother."

"That's where we met. She was a good friend."

"Friend?" Susie asked, her eyes narrowing. She remembered Taylor's idea that her mother and Phil might have had an affair. "This was before Nancy met my father, right?"

"They were married by then. I met your father after a performance and again at the cast party. We talked but never had a serious conversation. But your mother and I grew close and kept in touch after the play was over." He looked at Taylor. "I see that look. Let me be clear. Nancy and I never had an affair. There were only three true loves in my life: Theresa, acting, and politics. If I could live my life over again, I wouldn't have it any other way."

"Acting and politics? That's an odd combination."

"No, it's not. Ronald Reagan was once asked about that and said, 'How can a president *not* be an actor?' He was right, and it's true for all politicians, not just the ones at the top. What I found different about those two professions were the people I met, which is something I want to talk to you about. It's something Theresa knows about and it's something I've confessed to a priest. I don't feel guilty for what I did but many people would look down on me if they knew. Your mother was not one of those and I hope you won't be. Since I learned I'm dying, I've been looking for someone willing to listen to my secret with an open mind. I hope you'll be that person, you and your friends."

The word *dying* stuck in Susie's head and probably in everyone else's as well. They were all silent for a moment.

"We have something we want to discuss with you, too," Taylor told him. "Nancy had a last wish. That's why we're here. She told Susie to find Ginger's shoes. I discovered one in a closet in Susie's old Halsey Island house where Kyle and I now live, a dancer's shoe signed by Ginger Rogers. We're searching for its mate."

Phil closed his eyes, shook his head, and smiled from ear to ear. "Oh yes, I can tell you about that shoe and it has a great deal to do with the confession I have to make. Let me start from the beginning, back when I was a dirt poor actor with plenty of ambition. In those days I often volunteered to stuff envelopes for the campaigns of politicians I thought were going somewhere, hoping their money and power could help me. It did, but not in the way I imagined it would.

"A party was planned for a man running for a seat on the New Jersey General Assembly. They asked me to find live music for the event, someone inexpensive. It sounded difficult, but I had a friend named Jessica. She was an actress with a magnificent voice who played the guitar well enough and was desperate for money. She'd been taking roles in showcase and community theaters just for the exposure. Those roles paid nothing and kept her from working as a waitress. She was behind on her rent and eating mostly ramen noodles. She asked to borrow from me and a few of our other friends. I hated to say no, but I was almost as poor as she was. I guess our friends were in the same shape because everyone turned her down. The party gig paid little but Jessica took it anyway."

Chapter Nineteen

Thirty-Five Years Earlier

Phil felt a hand on his shoulder as he heard a voice say, "Wow!" He turned to see Mr. D, the man who had won the assembly seat and was that night's guest of honor. Mr. D leaned down, his mouth next to Phil's ear, and whispered, "That babe is amazing. Her voice is beautiful, and she's got a body to kill for. I can't believe you hired her for what we will pay."

"Jessica needs the money. She's an actress who thinks long term. You've got to think long *and* short if you're going to succeed. I've tried to tell her that but she doesn't listen."

"She's broke, huh?" Mr. D lowered his voice. "Maybe we can arrange something. I've got a conference coming up, in Indiana. I need eye candy. You know what I mean? I love my wife but she's getting old. For this trip, I need someone who will impress the other men. Could you get Jessica to agree to a long weekend with me? We would fly out there on Friday and return on Monday. Or maybe Tuesday, depending on how things go. If you can do that, I'd be grateful."

"Grateful?"

"That's right. If you help me, I'll be there when you need a favor. That's how things work."

"I can bring it up to her but that's all I can do."

"That should be enough. You tell her this. The conference is in three weeks. I'll pay two thousand if she comes with me and acts like my girlfriend for those few days. If what you said is right, that is money she needs. I'll throw in a few hundred for you, for setting this up. How's that sound?"

"Good." Phil stammered. "Yes, it sounds good. Should I tell Jessica to bring her guitar?"

Mr. D laughed. "No need for that. The only singing she'll be doing will be with me and she won't need a guitar for that."

He laughed again, grabbed and squeezed Phil's shoulder as he stood, then walked away.

Phil pinched his lower lip, wondering what he should do. His first inclination was not to tell Jessica any of this, just to let the offer die. But that didn't seem fair. She needed the money and had the right to make her own decision. He knew her well. They'd never been a couple, but they were good friends. They'd confided in each other many times over the years. He knew she'd had many boyfriends and a few one-night stands. She'd been on stage in her underwear in a production of *Noises Off* and naked in *The Robber Bridegroom*. She had what Phil considered a healthy attitude about sex. Did that include taking money for a weekend with Mr. D? He wasn't sure.

Jessica was about as sexy as any performer Phil had ever seen. She was wearing a gray tank top tied so her tight belly was exposed and her black jeans looked as if they'd been painted on. Strung through her belt loops was a shiny, metal sash that glimmered as she moved. To cap all of that, she wore a pair of polished boots, two necklaces, and a couple of bracelets. Jessica was every man's fantasy.

Mr. D's campaign had rented a van to bring over her guitar, amplifier, speakers, and microphone. They'd ridden to the party in the front and that's how Phil intended to bring her and her stuff home. After they disconnected everything and packed it in the back, he drove her to her apartment. On the way home, he told her about his conversation with Mr. D.

"I'm not a prostitute," she said.

"He knows you're not and I'm not a pimp. Those are not the questions here. Think of this as a role. If you want to play his girlfriend and all that entails, he'll pay you very well. It would be enough to handle your back rent at least."

Jessica blew her cheeks out then released the air slowly. "That's true." She rocked her head back and forth twice. "The guy is over fifty. I doubt he'll keep me up all night. It's just—I guess I've been brainwashed over the years."

"You think it's wrong?"

"Not for anyone else."

"But for you?"

"Maybe so. Oh God, I sound like a hypocrite."

"No, you don't. You shouldn't do something you feel uncomfortable doing."

"Like I said, he's over fifty. You know what I mean?"

"I do."

They both laughed.

They talked little for the rest of the ride. When they finished unpacking the van, Jessica turned to Phil, took his hands in hers, and said, "Give him my number and tell him to call me to set up the details."

"Then you'll do it?"

"Yes. It will solve all my problems for at least a few months. I think that's worth one weekend, don't you?"

"Your decision, not mine."

"I know."

A few days later, Phil received a check for three hundred dollars but he heard nothing from Jessica until a couple of months had passed. That's when he learned the weekend had been something unexpected. It had been fun. Jessica now had a regular relationship with Mr. D. He was paying her rent and buying her gifts. She'd called Phil for two reasons. The first was to thank him for setting her up with such a nice, wealthy man. The second was to ask if he could do something similar for her friend, Pamela.

Phil didn't know Pam personally but a couple of years earlier he had seen her play Lizzie in a small production of *The Rainmaker* in an East Village church. She made an impression. She probably had on basic stage makeup for the show, but he couldn't tell under the lights. Her hair was brown, and she wore a simple, cotton dress, white with a red floral pattern. She was the perfect farmer's daughter, strong and attractive without being overly sexual.

Her clean-cut appearance was one reason Phil hesitated, although he realized the actress could differ from the character she played. The other reason was his misconception about anyone who arranged these types of relationships. With Jessica and Mr. D, he had put together two friends who needed each other. This wasn't Pam's idea or the idea of any man who might pay for a night with her. If he took this step, he would be peddling flesh, not exactly a pimp but damn close.

"I'm not sure…" Phil's voice trailed off as he spoke. He swallowed, then started again. "I'm not sure I'm the right person."

"You did it for me," Jessica said. "How is Pam different?"

"I don't know her."

"Is that it?" She paused. "We can have lunch together, you, me, and Pam. I'll introduce you. At least agree to that, Phil. She told me she's having trouble making ends meet, and she also said she's jealous of what I have going for me."

They met at the Horn and Hardart automat. It wasn't a pricey meal, but it was still a surprise when Jessica offered to pick up the entire check. It was clear Jessica's finances were in good shape and Phil was certain Pam was aware of that fact.

The tables were square with four chairs. Jessica started to take the seat across from Phil but Pam touched Jessica's shoulder. They tried to be subtle. It was clear Pam did not want to sit next to Phil. When Pam spoke she looked down at the table rather than directly at either Phil or Jessica. She was constantly smoothing her skirt or fidgeting with her silverware. Phil knew the type, actresses who are comfortable on stage but nowhere else.

He could see why she would have trouble holding on to any of the jobs actors typically found to supplement their income. Yet her insecurity also meant she might have trouble performing in bed. Could he risk getting one of his wealthy contacts to pay for a night with someone so shy?

Phil called Jessica that evening and expressed his reservation about fixing Pam up with any of his contacts.

She uttered one sharp laugh. "You're worried about that? You've seen her on stage. She's a brilliant actress. She'll be fine. Most women fake it in bed at least some of the time."

"Really?"

"Sure. And if you don't believe me, you can spend some time alone with Pam before you set her up with someone else. She needs that money."

Wow, Phil thought. His first impulse was to say yes. It had been a while since he'd been with a woman, at least a couple of months. But this would be one more step to becoming a pimp. He had too much self-respect to let that happen.

Phil pulled away from the phone, looked up at the ceiling, took a deep breath, and brought it back to his ear. "No need for that," he told Jessica. "Tell Pam I'll see if I can come up with someone for her."

"You're a doll, Phil. I'll tell her you'll call."

"I'll call if I find someone. I'm not sure I can."

"Well, I'm sure."

* * *

Five years before Phil arranged the match between Jessica and Mr. D, he met Leah Blum in a dinner theater production of *Fiddler on the Roof*. Phil was a very athletic dancer, a talent that earned him a spot in the *To Life* scene. Leah was playing Hodel, the second daughter of Tevye. They got to know each other during rehearsals and dated twice. They stopped dating when Leah spoke what could have been a line from their show. She told Phil she didn't want to get serious with a gentile.

Phil was upset but their friendship endured. When *Fiddler* closed, they kept in touch through emails, even after Leah married Bob Abrams. In her most recent email, Phil learned Leah had a serious health issue.

Phil,

I need someone to talk to and I chose you because you're a good friend.

I've been diagnosed with stage four breast cancer. It's spread to my lymph system and from there to my lungs and liver. I was stupid. I discovered the lump when there were still six months to go on the road with Anything Goes. Despite the length of time, I waited to see my doctor. When I did, she told me the bad news. She said it would probably have been too far along even if I had acted quickly, but I think she said that just to make me feel better. I'm going to do everything I can to fight this but the prognosis is not good.

The touring schedule called for a year away from home. I worried about the strain this would put on my marriage but I knew Bob loved me. I was certain I could win him back even if he met someone else while I was away.

But I didn't count on this. I'm sick and weak and haven't been able to get through this pain and trouble without taking my anger out on him. I find I yell about the smallest things and cry at unreasonable times.

Also, there is our time alone. There is no intimacy and there's no way there can be, not with me. Bob's a good man but he's not cut out to be a caretaker. I can see he's stressed, but it is impossible for me to stop being the sick person this disease has created.

There's a reason I'm writing to you instead of one of my female friends. I need a man's perspective. I don't want to keep hurting him but I also don't want to pull away when I need him the most.

Neither one of us is religious. I know that. But I could use prayers.

Your friend,
Leah

Phil wasn't sure Leah knew Jessica, but it seemed they'd been in touch. Why else would she write such a personal note? He read it over again. "There is no intimacy…" "he's not cut out to be…" It was as if Leah was asking him to connect her husband with someone who could give him a break from cancer and her impending death.

Pam seemed the perfect solution. From what he could tell, she wasn't looking for a permanent relationship, just a way to pay her bills.

The next day he called Bob Abrams. "I was hoping we could meet for dinner. I'm buying."

"Why?"

"Your wife asked me to. She wants me to talk to you."

"That's what I thought, but I don't need your help."

"I didn't say I could help, but Leah feels you need to talk to someone. She told you we're friends, right?"

"Yeah. She talks about you sometimes. You two used to date."

"That was a long time ago. Being a couple didn't work out, but being friends did. That's why she came to me. I'm the friend who does what she asks, especially if it's important. And that's what this is—important."

"You think it will make her feel better?"

"I know it will. She's worried about you."

"She's the one with cancer."

"Leah's the one with the disease but you're going through as much stress or maybe even more than what she is. That's always true with caretakers."

"All right. I'll meet with you. Where?"

"You choose."

"Do you know The Windlass?"

"Of course. I'll see you there tomorrow night. Is 6:00 all right?"

"Make it 5:30, before the rush. You buy the dinner. I'll buy the drinks."

"Sounds fair."

Phil arrived early so he could get a table. He parked in the back and walked around to the front to go in. He loved The Windlass. The walls were stained dark brown with nautical hangings and pictures. The windows on one side looked out over the lake. Phil was fortunate and got a booth on the lakeside. He ordered a beer and sat there until Bob arrived about a half hour later. Phil asked him what he wanted to drink. He said scotch, so Phil switched what he was drinking and ordered two J & B's, on the rocks.

"Why did you want to meet here?" Phil asked.

"I live in Sparta which is where I have my shop but my father had a house near River Styx with lakefront property and a boathouse. I used to paddle our canoe under the bridge and into Crescent Cove most every day, even when the weather was turning cold. It was my safe place. I'd go there to think about everything from school to girls to God. When I grew up and got a place of my own, I didn't move far. I would still go back to my dad's house until he and my mom were both gone. After that, I sold it. I used the money to start my machine shop. I've been thinking about buying another house somewhere on the lake, one that I could use in the warm weather. It may seem silly to have a summer house and a winter house so close to each other but I thought it would be something Leah and I would both like. Then this disease hit her and now I'm not sure. She's so weak she rarely gets out of bed. She's going to fight her way through it and I'm confident she'll win. But maybe I'll wait on the house. Maybe I'll buy her a summer place when she's licked the disease and can appreciate it."

Phil knew Bob was being optimistic. Leah's cancer was not something she was going to kick, not without a miracle. "Have you thought about renting? I could picture Leah sitting by the lake, watching the boats go by. It might get her mind off the pain."

"Maybe." Bob paused. "I'll think about that." He paused again and sighed. "I'm glad Leah sent you my way. She's right. I need someone to talk to. Life is hard for my wife but sometimes I want to focus on me and the problems I have. It's hard to take care of her while I'm still running my shop. We have a part-time nurse who helps while I'm at work. She bathes Leah and cuts her hair, but I'm the one who is there every day and I'm tired."

"Are you lonely, too?"

"I suppose lonely is the right word. How do you complain about the idiot who cut you off on Route 46 when the person you're talking to will never drive a car again? It's hard, especially if you love the person."

Phil looked down at his near-empty scotch glass. He fidgeted with it, swirling the water from the melted ice, then looked up at Bob. *Pam would be perfect*, he thought.

The waitress came by to take their orders. Phil ordered the chicken cacciatore and Bob said, "I'll have the same."

The meal was good, and the conversation had no periods of uncomfortable silence. It was clear Bob enjoyed having the chance to express his feelings out loud. When they were done with the main meal, they each had a dish of ice cream and a cup of black coffee.

Bob picked up his cup and finished the last of his coffee. "We all have to die. I know that. But I don't want to think about it 24/7, you know what I mean?"

Phil didn't answer. Instead of listening he was contemplating his next move. "I can't stay any longer," Phil told his newfound friend, "but I'd like to schedule another dinner with you."

"I don't know what *you're* getting out of this but I'm glad Leah sent you that email." He smiled. "How about next week, Tuesday, maybe? Six o'clock?"

"Sounds good."

"I'll pay this time."

"No need."

"Yes, there is. Paying will make me feel better."

"I can't argue with that."

They walked out together, then got into their separate cars. Phil drove back to his apartment and immediately called Jessica.

Phil was feeling light-headed, almost giddy. The meeting with Bob Abrams had gone better than he'd thought it could. Jessica picked up his call and without even saying hello he told her, "I think he'll be a good match for Pam. Leah was concerned about his physical needs but I believe he simply needs someone to talk to. He's lonely. He's the boss at his machine shop. That puts him on a different level than the people he supervises. He can't open up to them in that situation and beyond those people, he doesn't seem to have anyone to talk to. His wife's cancer leaves him feeling guilty if he thinks about his own problems. It was easy to get him to talk to me but I think he needs a woman, someone sensitive enough to show her emotion and to get him to show his."

"He sounds perfect for Pam."

"Yes. Here's my plan. We're scheduled to meet again. I'd like to bring Pam with me. When we're there, I'll make some excuse to leave them alone. I'll head to the restroom or say I have to make a phone call. When they only have each other to talk to, they'll hit it off. The only problem I see is I haven't discussed money with him yet."

"Money you want? Or what he'll need to pay Pam?"

Phil wet his lips. "Uh…Both."

"You've seen Pam. It won't take long for this relationship to get physical. After that, he'll pay anything to keep it going."

"You're probably right there, although each step brings me closer to feeling like a pimp."

"We've got a good business going here, you with your rich friends and me knowing which actresses are behind in their bills. But money is only a part of it. We're matchmakers, like in *Fiddler*. There's nothing wrong with what we're doing."

"I guess you're right."

"Of course I am. Listen. I'll speak to Pam. If she agrees we can move forward with your plan. I'll cover the dinners and pay your portion upfront. I'm sure she'll pay me back once she's got her debts covered. We're doing good here. We're helping people in need."

* * *

"I'm not sure about this," Pam told Jessica when she called. "I don't mean to criticize your situation, Jess. It has worked out well for you, but I don't want to be a kept woman."

"I hate that term."

"I don't know what else to call it. Mr. D pays your rent and keeps food on your table, right?"

"It's an arrangement. That's all."

Pam cleared her throat. "I think it's like any other permanent relationship. When you tie yourself to one man, you limit your freedoms."

"Limit?" Jessica ran her left hand through her hair. "It's exactly the opposite. If you establish the right relationship, you'll be free to audition at any time. You can pick up roles in regional theater or touring companies, gigs that will take you away from New York. You can't do that if you have to work to pay your bills."

"So what you're saying is, either way, we have to give up some of our freedoms and this would be the lesser of two evils?"

"Sure. And from what Phil says, the main thing this man will want is a shoulder to cry on. All you have to do is act concerned and caring. You're an actress. You can do that."

"All right. I'll meet the guy. We'll see where it goes from there."

* * *

The second dinner with Bob went even better than the first. Pam showed up dressed in a long-sleeved dress with a high neckline and a midi-length skirt. The dress was black with bright colors splashed across it from just below the shoulders to the hem of the skirt, showing less and less of the black background as the pattern went lower as if it was dripping down her body. The design looked like a Jackson Pollock painting and the dress fit like the skin of a shedding snake, tight in some places and loose in others.

Pam appeared conservative but also seductive, like Michelle Pfeiffer. She was five foot seven or eight, thin with small breasts, like a model. Her face was covered with freckles but they were soft and light. Her skin seemed right with her dark red hair and green eyes.

"Pam's a friend of mine," Phil told Bob as they sat across from him. "I hope you don't mind. I asked her to come along." Bob shrugged as Phil continued speaking. "She's an actress who lives in New York. She will be the first to admit she's still struggling with her career but that worked to our favor. Pam never turns down a free meal." Phil looked at her. "Right?" She smiled and nodded, then Phil returned his focus on Bob. "That's the reason she agreed to come but not the reason I asked her. Pam is a superb listener and I think she's someone who can help you deal with the stress of your life."

They talked more, mostly about what they'd like to eat and drink but also about Pam's drive from the city. Traffic on Route 80 wasn't horrible, but it's never great. Then Phil excused himself to use the men's room.

When he returned to the table, they were discussing a recent audition for *Spring Awakening* that had not gone well for Pam. More accurately, Pam was talking about it while Bob was listening. Neither of them paid any attention to Phil as he took a seat. Apparently, Pam was too young for the adult roles and too old for the teenage parts.

Bob's head jerked back. "Too old?" He shook his head. "You look young."

"Not young enough but that might not have been it. They never tell you how you did. They just don't call you unless they want you. It's always the same."

They seemed comfortable with each other so Phil leaned toward Bob. "Now, tell me and Pam what you've been through this week."

Bob blew out his cheeks before answering. He looked at Phil, avoiding eye contact with Pam. "Leah had an awful week. She was experiencing pain in some parts of her body and numbness in others."

Pam leaned forward and touched her chin. "Has your wife tried laetrile? I have a friend with cancer. She told me that helped her more than the drugs the doctors gave her."

"We're not into alternative medicine."

"Check with her doctor if you want to. Laetrile is hard to get in America, but I could talk to my friend if you want me to. She has a source."

Bob looked at Phil then back at Pam and pressed his lips together. "Thanks. I'll think about it."

The conversation was going well so Phil excused himself, saying he wanted to ask at the bar if they had a bottle of Auburn Road Red. He spoke with the bartender for a few minutes, glancing back at Bob and Pam every so often to see if they were getting along. They were. When he returned Pam said she needed to use the restroom. This gave Phil a chance to talk to Bob alone. "She's willing to meet with you regularly."

"Like a therapist?"

"Exactly, like a therapist." Phil smiled. "Like most struggling actresses, Pam's strapped for cash, so you might have to help her out there somewhat. But she'd be a good shoulder to cry on. Remember, Leah loves you. Whatever eases your pain will help her, too."

* * *

A month after Bob's wife passed, he and Phil met again. They were back at the Windlass but not for dinner this time, just drinks and the opportunity for Bob to tell Phil how everything had worked out.

His voice cracked when he spoke of Leah. "She smiled and told me I looked more at ease than I had in a long time." His chin was trembling. Phil could see he was trying to hold back tears. "She knew I was seeing someone. She was dying, and that's how she responded." Bob leaned across the table, looked into Phil's eyes, and spoke in a lower voice. "I don't know if I could have gotten through this without Pam's help."

Phil was fairly sure their relationship was no longer platonic, and that belief seemed to be confirmed when Bob handed him a check for two thousand dollars, one for him and one for Jessica. Bob and Pam were a perfect match and Leah died at peace knowing that someone would be there for Bob.

* * *

Five years after Phil and Jessica set up Bob and Pam, Mr. D left Jessica. It was an amicable separation. Mr. D wanted someone new and Jessica's financial issues were solved. She had made plenty of money from the business she shared with Phil, much of which she invested in stocks and bonds. Jessica found another actress for her ex, someone ten years younger. This was tricky for her because their matchmaking was now focused less on long-term relationships and more on one-night stands. Also, they had switched from actresses to housewives who were looking for excitement and less financial dependency on their husbands.

Phil was concerned about the way their business had changed. He worried he was less of a matchmaker and more of the pimp he'd feared becoming. He was also concerned about the women they were working with. The switch from financially strapped young women to bored housewives meant the women and men often traveled in the same circles. So far it hadn't been a problem but he could see a situation where a woman might attend a party with her husband and be introduced to someone she'd been intimate with. If that happened, everything might fall apart and there could be legal ramifications.

Phil and Jessica decided it was a good time to shut down their enterprise. Jessica wanted to concentrate more on her acting career and Phil had fallen in love with a woman he'd met while working with the Eliot Spitzer campaign for governor of New York.

Phil told Theresa he was giving up acting to concentrate on politics. He did not tell her how he'd earned his fortune, since that would also be over, and he didn't feel the need to complicate things. He did plan to tell her eventually but that could wait a long time.

Chapter Twenty

The first time Phil kissed Nancy was awkward. He had just proposed to Theresa and Nancy was married to Scott but this wasn't an affair, not even a tiny one. The kiss was called for in the script of *Romantic Comedy*, so neither of the spouses felt betrayed. Still, it is hard to kiss someone without feeling something and everyone knew that.

Although Phil had made most of his money by arranging encounters, he still felt uncomfortable kissing a woman he hardly knew. Fortunately, this was supposed to be an artless kiss that would lead to disappointment in bed for both the characters they were playing. There was another scene they would have to work on later, one where she would be lying on him and they would be enjoying the kiss. When they reached that section, he would try to imagine he was holding Theresa instead of Nancy. That might work but it would be difficult because their bodies were different. Nancy was taller and had less meat on her bones.

By the time the curtain fell on their final performance, Phil and Nancy had become good friends, good enough that he opened up to her about how he'd made his fortune. He still hadn't told Theresa. Phil didn't know if the kisses had helped or hurt his friendship with Nancy but he wanted to continue to see her.

There was a cast party after the last performance which was the first time Nancy met Theresa. Theresa's appearance surprised Nancy. Theresa was short, about five foot two, and stocky, with a round face. She had wavy, brown hair, like an unclipped poodle which she wore parted in the middle and long, a few inches below her shoulders. Theresa looked nice, but she was not what Nancy expected.

When the party was over Phil and Theresa approached Nancy and Scott to say goodbye. Phil held out his hand, apparently to shake Nancy's, but he pulled her into a hug.

"I'll miss working with you," he told her.

"Me too."

"Really?"

"Yes."

"Then I'd like to ask you something."

"What?"

"I'm planning to run for mayor of Mt. Arlington."

"You told me that."

"Would you like to help with my campaign?"

"Sure, but how? I know nothing about politics."

"You would do things like addressing envelopes or canvassing."

"Canvassing?"

Phil grinned. "You'd be going door to door, handing out pamphlets and telling people how wonderful I am."

Nancy laughed as she nodded. "I'd like to do that."

Phil glanced at Scott and Theresa who were standing close to the front door. She was looking down. He was shaking his head.

"Does this work pay?" Scott asked.

"No, it's volunteer work. Although I could pay a small salary if I made Nancy a supervisor."

She held both her hands up. "I could never supervise but I would like to take part. Can I bring Scott?"

Phil was about to say "Yes," but Scott spoke first.

"Don't volunteer me," Scott told his wife. "This is not *my* thing."

"All right." She turned back to Phil. "Then can I bring a friend?"

"Of course."

* * *

The following Thursday, Nancy brought Mary Olsen to Phil's house where Theresa greeted them. Phil's wife was dressed conservatively in a black dress with small white spots. The dress had a midi-length, ruffled skirt. Above the waist, it was baggy with long sleeves.

Theresa led the two women to the dining room where Phil was waiting with four others. Given what Nancy knew of him and his matchmaking business, she'd expected the woman he'd fallen for to look more like one of these. They were all tall, thin, and as sexy as Bo Derek.

Nancy recognized two of the women from an audition she'd attended for the musical, *Barnum*. Nancy hadn't been cast, probably because of her poor dancing, but had attended a performance and noticed they were both in the chorus. She didn't remember their names, so she feigned ignorance and waited for Phil or Theresa to introduce them. She assumed these women had been among the ones Phil had set up with wealthy men, although she was certain he knew plenty of actresses who weren't involved with that business.

"This is Nancy and her friend Mary," Theresa announced. "And these young ladies are Karen, Ann, Linda, and Sandra." The women were gathered around a table on which there were stacks of postcards, a couple of rolls of stamps, and a few sheets of paper with printed names and addresses. Their task was simple. They needed to copy a pre-written message about Phil's qualifications onto postcards. After that, they would stamp the cards and address them from the lists of names and addresses.

It didn't take long before Nancy memorized the message, which sped up the task. Mary was also writing quickly, but the others were slower. They kept chatting about shows they'd been in and upcoming auditions.

Chapter Twenty-One

2022

"That was the only time I met your mother," Phil told Kyle. He turned to Susie. "But I met with *your* mother many times after that. She was desperate for something and she knew I could help."

"What did she want?"

"That's not for me to say."

Susie's face turned red. "Not for you to say?" Her voice was loud and cracking. "Was my mother one of your prostitutes?"

"None of my women were prostitutes."

Susie narrowed her eyes. "Right."

"They were housewives and actresses."

"My mother was both those things."

"True. But I helped her differently and she paid me for what I did."

Susie thought about the $7,000 listed on her parents' old tax forms. That had to be for something her father knew about. What could it have been?

"Susie. I understand your concern." The voice was Theresa's. Everyone turned to see her standing by the dining room door. "Phil was done with all of that when I met him. Trust him. Your mother needed something else."

Phil sighed. "I had your birth certificate changed." He shook his head.

"That's all?"

"It's all I'm going to say."

Theresa crossed her arms and narrowed her eyes. "You can help her more than that."

Phil paused. "I'll give you a name."

"A name?"

Taylor cleared her throat. "You haven't told us what happened to the shoe. Can this person help with that?"

"I suppose that is what you're after, isn't it?" Phil laughed. "I connected Nancy with a woman who could help her. That's when Nancy split the pair of shoes. She gave one to that woman and kept one for herself. It was a symbol of their connection. The woman died five years ago but her daughter's alive. The daughter's name is Brooke Bevans and goes by the nickname BB. It's her name I said I would give you and now I have. She probably has the shoe but what's most important is she can tell you what her mother did. That's why it's her story to tell."

Susie got nothing more from Phil Robinson, except BB's address. She lived alone, in a one bedroom apartment in Montclair.

* * *

Susie was sitting at her desk in Dr. Harris' office the morning after the visit with Phil and Theresa Robinson. She had trouble concentrating. She was thinking about what Phil Robinson had confessed. His words concerned her because her mother had asked him for something and had paid him a significant amount of money when he did it.

Nancy must have known about Phil's matchmaking history, but by the time they met he'd been out of the business. So what could she have wanted from him? Kidnapping might cost that much but she couldn't picture her parents doing anything that awful. Changing the birth certificate was a possibility but she couldn't understand why it could cost $7,000. That was a lot of money back then.

Another thing was worrying her. Lately, when she was with Danny, she was thinking of Kyle, which made her feel guilty. She could tell their relationship was going nowhere.

Susie's workspace was at the end of a hall that ran alongside the five treatment rooms and the X-ray lab. There was a wall between her desk and the waiting room, with a large window so Susie could greet and check in the patients as they arrived.

When the phone rang, it was generally one of Dr. Harris' patients either scheduling or canceling an appointment but that morning she was surprised to receive a call from Taylor. "I need to talk to you. Could we meet when you're done with work? I'll buy you dinner."

"Today?"

"If it's convenient for you."

"We close at five but you better make it around five-thirty. Sometimes Dr. Harris runs late with the last patient."

Susie's stomach fluttered as she hung up the phone. An elderly woman who was standing at her window asked her to check when she'd last had X-rays. She knew the woman but couldn't remember her name. She asked her to spell it. That trick made a bad situation worse because the woman's name wasn't hard to spell. It was Wilson.

Susie was not having a good day. It was as if her mind was caught in a whirlpool. *Was Taylor thinking of this dinner as a date?* Susie was feeling enough guilt over her relationship with Danny. She didn't want Taylor to think there was a chance for anything beyond friendship.

When the clock said five-twenty-five, Susie went to the restroom. She fixed her makeup, and used a small brush she carried in her purse to make her hair look halfway decent.

Susie's relationship with Danny had grown old and somewhat boring even before she reconnected with Kyle. She had looked at Kyle more than she should have and Taylor might be looking at her. She remembered a line from the musical, *Hair*, when a character denies being homosexual but says, "Well, I wouldn't kick Mick Jagger out of my bed." Susie laughed over that thought.

* * *

Taylor was waiting in a green Mini Cooper with a black top. Susie hadn't seen this car previously, since Kyle had driven his BMW when they'd dropped in on Nancy's old friends. Two things surprised Susie when she stepped out of the office. The first was the polished green and black car, of course, and how good Taylor looked in it. Taylor was wearing a black top with elbow-length sleeves. The second was the person sitting in the passenger seat. Taylor had brought a friend, a woman who appeared to be in her fifties or sixties. It was hard to tell. She was overweight and dressed in a man-tailored button shirt, orange with a black pattern. Her black hair was cut unevenly, short on her left and long on her right. Susie could not see what either woman was wearing below the waist until she was next to the car. Taylor was in a knee-length, black-and-white skirt. One of her sandal-clad feet was resting on the brake pedal. Her friend was wearing baggy mom jeans

Taylor opened the car window, tilted her head toward the woman next to her, and grinned. "This is Izzy Evans." She then nodded at Susie. "And this is Susie, Nancy Walsh's daughter."

With that simple introduction, what was happening became clear to Susie. Taylor had been doing some research on her own and had found someone else who knew her mother.

"When I learned your mother was in an early production of *Last Summer at Bluefish Cove*, I thought some of the other cast members might be around. Izzy is the only one I found. She played Donna in the show where your mother played Eva. I think you should hear what she has to say."

Izzy pushed her shoulders back, lifted her chin, and laughed. "Nancy was the only straight woman in the cast, which was funny since Eva falls for Lil and Nancy was convincing. I was ten years younger than her, in my prime so to speak, but I wanted Nancy and so did all the other women. There's something special about being someone's first."

Susie blew out a breath. "My mother was a talented actress."

"We were all talented, a special cast."

"Let's head over to the restaurant," Taylor said. "We can get drinks and talk while we wait for our meals."

"All right," Susie told her. "Can we caravan over? I don't want to leave my car here."

Taylor led Susie to a wine bar in Hanover. It was noisy, but they took a table against a wall where they could talk. They ordered a bottle of Royal Post, a California Rose, to drink while they looked over the menu and Izzy started talking about the Nancy she had once known, an actress in her late thirties, happy for any role she could get.

Chapter Twenty-Two

Thirty-Three Years Earlier

It was the read-through, their first get-together as a cast. Ten women were sitting around two folding tables, the eight actresses in the cast of *Last Summer at Bluefish Cove* along with the director and the stage manager. Nancy had been in plays where they had to circle the chairs because there were twenty-some actors involved but this was an intimate show.

Nancy's character, Eva, was the second on stage. Lil was the first. By the end of the play, they would be in love.

Lil was played by Olivia Bennett, a tall, stunning blue-eyed woman with long dark hair reaching at least six inches below her shoulders. It was full and wavy and as close to being black as brown hair could be. Nancy understood how someone of either gender could fall for Olivia. On the other hand, Nancy had pale skin and thin brown hair. Her only outstanding feature was her eyes which were almost as dark as Olivia's hair. Was that enough for Lil to fall for Eva? Nancy would have to make sure it was.

The reading went well and the other actresses seemed nice, except for the young woman who was to play Donna. She made some wisecracks that were more rude than funny. Yet the others did not seem to mind. Perhaps they were pleased she was staying in character.

Dawn Jacobs, the director, made a few comments after the read-through was done. Then, as everyone else was leaving, she asked Nancy to stay behind. "I want to go over my expectations for your character."

"You weren't happy with my reading?"

"You were fine. I just need to talk to you."

Nancy slumped back into her chair. *Why would Dawn want to speak to her alone?*

When everyone else was gone, Dawn said, "You are the only straight woman in this cast. Did you know that?"

"I...I had a feeling that was true." Nancy's voice quavered. She was worried. She could not figure out where this conversation was going.

"I had a choice and I hope I made the right one. Eva is like you at the beginning of our story. She's never been with a woman. At the end of the play, Eva is in love with a woman. A lesbian might carry that part off but struggle with the first act. A straight woman is going to have a harder time with the second half. I probably would have gone with a woman who understands gay love if I hadn't seen you in *Two for the Seasaw.*"

"You saw that? It was a showcase. We ran one weekend."

"True, but I was there, and you were fabulous."

"That play is about a heterosexual affair."

"But a complicated one. If you can handle that part, I believe you can handle this. I'm going to ask you to prove me right by putting your heart into our show."

"I always do that."

Dawn nodded then said, "I want more than what you always do. Get to know Olivia well. Spend time with her after rehearsals. Go for drinks. Talk to each other. Understand the way she feels."

Nancy took in a deep breath and let it out slowly. "Make her fall in love with me?"

"All I'm saying is make it real. The show is everything."

Nancy did what Dawn requested of her. After each rehearsal, members of the cast would go out for drinks. Nancy joined them and tried to sit next to Olivia as often as possible. That was easy to do because they were on stage together a lot. They could talk about blocking, reactions, and timing in their scenes. There were no periods of awkward silence.

Olivia walked tall and forcefully, appearing as dominating as Ellen Ripley in *Alien,* but she was sweet. Once Nancy got to know Olivia, she enjoyed her company. Maybe Dawn had known they would click as friends. Nancy could see why their roles made getting along important. Kissing and caressing someone you don't like would be something akin to lying down for a nap in a thorn bush.

As they grew closer, Nancy worried Olivia would seek physical intimacy and had come up with several excuses, most of which were true. Yet, Olivia seemed to enjoy their platonic friendship as much as Nancy did.

Olivia often asked questions about Nancy's relationship with her husband, especially about his reaction to her choice to be an actress. Working in the theater requires a lot of time and can interfere with a couple's intimacy. Apparently, Olivia had just broken up with a woman she'd dated for five years. The woman had been her hairdresser. Now Olivia was alone and also needed to find someone else to cut her hair. For an actress, the second problem was a big deal.

One day Olivia opened up to Nancy about something she hadn't expected. She cleared her throat. "I really like Izzy," she said in a soft voice, leaning forward so only Nancy could hear.

"You mean *like* as in you want to date her?"

"Yes. I think I could be good for her."

That was a shock. The two women hadn't said more than a few words to each other when they weren't on stage. Also, Olivia was Nancy's age, at least ten years older than Izzy, which complicated the situation.

Olivia bit her lower lip. "You think I have a chance?"

Nancy wasn't about to bring up the age thing. "You're a beautiful woman," she told Olivia. "If she isn't seeing anyone else I don't know why you wouldn't—have a chance that is."

"Can you help me?"

"How?"

"Talk me up."

Olivia was asking Nancy to be her wingman as if they were a couple of frat boys. It seemed strange, especially for someone who appeared to be so confident. Her breakup must have hurt a lot.

Nancy slid toward the aisle, then stood up. "I'll tell you what. I'll go ask her to join us. Then I'll make some excuse and leave you two alone. After that, it's up to you."

Izzy smiled and nodded when Nancy suggested she join them. She followed Nancy back to the booth but instead of sitting next to Olivia, Izzy squeezed in next to Nancy.

Olivia was a stunning beauty, much more attractive than Nancy. At least, that was Nancy's opinion. It was apparently not one shared by Izzy. The younger woman kept touching Nancy's arm and even leaned her head against Nancy's shoulder a few times. It was true some lesbians liked the thrill of chasing straight women and perhaps Izzy was one of those. Trying to be Olivia's wingman was not working out well for Nancy. She had to get Izzy's focus back on the woman sitting across the table.

"Did you know Olivia was born in Block, Tennessee? That's a rural town in the Appalachian Mountains. She's part Cherokee." Nancy switched from Izzy to Olivia. "Is that where you got your gorgeous hair?"

Olivia smiled and looked at Izzy as she answered Nancy's question. "I use conditioner and sheep placenta. I guess I got lucky with what I inherited but I work to get my locks looking the best they can."

Izzy laughed. "So that's your secret. Sheep placenta?"

Nancy said, "I've heard of that but never tried it."

"How the hell did someone discover sheep placenta is good for hair?" Izzy asked while wrinkling her nose. "Did some unfortunate farmer's wife get the stuff all over her when she was pulling a lamb out of a Ewe? Was that the eureka moment?"

"I don't know about any moment but it works."

Nancy tried to change the subject. "The way she made her way to New York is absolutely amazing. Tell her, Olivia."

Izzy rolled her eyes. "Please don't. I get so sick of rags-to-riches stories. It seems like every woman I meet has one."

Izzy was full of snarky remarks but Olivia liked her, anyway. Nancy hoped her attraction was based on more than Izzy's physical appearance. In one scene, most of the women come out in bathing suits. Everyone is in modest one-pieces except for Izzy whose character is dressed in a yellow bikini. She wears it so well she could have been posing for the annual *Sports Illustrated* swimsuit issue.

"How about you, Izzy," Nancy asked. "Do you have a story?"

"I do. I've been on stage since I was one of the workhouse children in *Oliver!* when I was seven years old. My father was a stagehand, so I grew up in theaters."

Nancy let out a short bark of a laugh. "What a fun childhood!"

Izzy smiled. "It was. We were children. How successful you needed to be to work in a Broadway theater did not impress us, but we loved the music, the dark places where we could play hide and seek, and the dance numbers, which we tried to imitate. Some of those kids were talented dancers, very athletic."

"You say *we*?"

"Yes. There were always other kids around, the children of stagehands, like I was, and the children of the actors. I made plenty of friends but they moved on when the various shows would close. I had to make new ones when my father got his next job. I went to the theaters a lot because he was a single dad. My mom left us when I was four."

Nancy felt an ache in her chest and was about to tell Izzy how sad she was to hear about her mother. But Olivia spoke first. "Could you have used any of those friends to help kick off your career?"

"Like everyone in this profession, I use all my connections as much as I can. I've landed a couple of roles through some of those childhood acquaintances but not as many as you would think."

At first, Olivia's response to Izzy's comment about her mother seemed heartless but Izzy appeared content to keep the conversation focused on professional rather than personal talk. In fact, from that point on she seemed to pay much more attention to Olivia than she did to Nancy.

During the rehearsals, Izzy had seemed like a sharp-witted but self-centered person, someone like Dorothy Parker. Yet, Nancy was seeing her serious side. Izzy was much more mature than she had believed.

It only took about a half hour of listening to Olivia and Izzy talk for Nancy to realize she could slip out without being missed all that much. She made up an excuse. She said she was returning to New Jersey to spend the night with her husband instead of staying in the motel room she had in Brooklyn during the rehearsal period. Neither Olivia nor Izzy seemed to care. They just wanted to be alone.

Nancy's involvement with Olivia and Izzy did not end after that night. Now that they were a couple, they were discovering things about each other they hadn't known. Most of those things were nice, but some were causes of irritation. Nancy became a confidant.

Olivia liked to spend time with a friend she'd known for years but Izzy was jealous, claiming she would find a friend of her own if Olivia refused to give up hers. They brought that problem to Nancy who suggested they invite this friend to dinner so Izzy could get to know her, too. That worked well.

Olivia wanted to get rid of one of their apartments and live together to save money but Izzy didn't want to move so fast. Nancy agreed with Izzy on this one. They'd only known each other a few weeks. Overall, the problems were minor and helped Nancy become a good friend to both of them.

Nancy was Olivia's age and older than Izzy but because of the way they depended on her and the advice she offered, they both called her "Mom."

Chapter Twenty-Three

2022

Susie ran her fingers through her hair, tucking it behind her ears. "My mom was an exceptional mother. It's nice knowing others saw that in her as well."

Izzy smiled. "Olivia and I stayed together for decades after that show—until she passed away five years ago. The first few years are always difficult for any couple, getting used to living life with and for someone else. Your mother helped us past those early conflicts that seem so silly in hindsight. We raised a daughter together, Olivia and I. And she turned out to be a wonderful person. I believe you're going to meet her. In fact, that's why I'm talking to you now. When I heard from Taylor that Phil had given you BB's name and address I knew I had to talk to you first."

Taylor raised an eyebrow. "You're saying this woman, BB, is your child?"

Izzy nodded. "Olivia carried her and birthed her but she is as much mine as she ever was Olivia's. I love her and I believe Olivia still does, too, from her place in heaven."

"I don't understand," Susie told Izzy. "I appreciate how important my mother was to you but what does your daughter have to do with me?"

"She has the shoe. Your mother gave it to Olivia who left it to BB. She had it listed in her will. That's how important it was to her."

When they left the wine bar, Susie said goodbye, then watched as Izzy and Taylor headed for Taylor's Mini Cooper. Susie turned to walk to her Camry, which she had parked a couple of spaces away, when Taylor stopped and shouted to her. "Can you come back to the lake tonight?"

"Don't you have to drop Izzy off?"

"You can either follow us or head over to Bridge Marina and wait there. I think it's important we talk over some of what we learned about your mother and BB. I believe we're getting close to what you're supposed to discover."

There are so many things I've already learned, Susie thought. *Could we be close to the end of this search?*

She drove toward the marina rather than following Taylor but along the way she decided she needed to deal with Danny. Susie couldn't keep her feelings from him any longer. She pulled into the parking lot of a ShopRite, found a spot at the edge of the lot with no other cars nearby, pulled out her phone, and called him.

"Hey Susie. What's up?"

She glanced around one more time to be sure no one could hear her. "I'm on my way to the lake. Taylor and Kyle invited me to spend another night."

"That sounds nice. You want me to meet you there?"

"No. That isn't why I'm calling—not exactly."

"Oh?"

Susie looked at a lady about twenty yards away, unloading groceries into the trunk of a white sedan. "I've been giving some thought to us. We need to have a conversation."

"Us?"

"Yes…where things are going." She took in a breath then added, "And if we're right for each other."

"Oh no. Are you breaking up with me?"

"Not exactly. Oh…that's wrong. I suppose I am but listen to me, please. We've had a wonderful time together. It's just that I'm not sure I should be tied down to one person."

"Tied?" His voice was getting louder. "It's that damn search, isn't it? Your mom was just a B-list actress. Why pay any attention to her last wish?"

"She wasn't B-list."

"Whatever you say. You know everything, don't you? Susie Walsh, the perfect person. Yet here you are breaking up with me over the phone." She could hear him breathing hard. "Well, let me tell you the truth. You are a self-centered bit…" His voice faded on the last word but she knew what he meant.

"I'm sorry," she told him. "I'm sorry Danny, I didn't want this to be hard and I'm still going to see you. I mean, you're still going to be our supplier at work, right?"

"I'm a pro and I'll be there. Dr. Harris is a friend of mine. He will not let a shallow, rude receptionist affect our business arrangement." He paused but she could hear him breathing hard. "I'll deal with you only as much as I have to. You'll be surprised by how fast I'll get over you."

Danny hung up. Susie held on to the phone for a moment more, feeling empty and numb. But she'd done what had to be done, and she would not let his reaction affect her plans. She took a deep breath, grasped the steering wheel with both hands, and told herself, "Now clear your mind." She took another breath, let it out slowly, turned the car on, and pulled back onto Route 15.

As she drove, she pushed Danny out of her thoughts and turned them to Izzy, Olivia, and the child they raised. She also thought about her mother's role as their confidant. Most of what Taylor had hypothesized seemed wrong. Izzy and Phil both portrayed Nancy as a fairly normal suburban housewife who was kind and caring, but would BB agree with them? Susie needed to meet with her as soon as possible.

When she reached the marina, she parked her car and headed out to the end of the pier. Kyle's boat was tied in its dock slip. This surprised her. If Kyle was on the island, the boat should have been with him and he would have been waiting for Taylor to call so he could pick them up. Perhaps he was working late, and the plan was for Taylor to take the boat to Halsey Island and wait for Kyle's call.

She walked out to the end of the pier, took her shoes off, rolled up her long jeans as well as she could, sat on the edge of the dock, and dipped her feet in the water. It was late August and fairly cool but she enjoyed dipping her feet in and swishing them around to make waves. This reminded her of her childhood on the island. She spent a lot of time alone back then. Heather Jordan had been the only other child her age who spent summers on the island and they hadn't gotten along well. That's one reason her mom invited Kyle up so often.

Susie lifted her head to watch a couple of boats go under Brady Bridge and noted how few there were compared to the constant line during midsummer. She liked the lake late in the season. It was peaceful.

"Hello, Susie." She turned at the sound of a man's voice.

Kyle was standing behind her. "Taylor called to say you're spending another night with us. That's nice." He sat down beside her and started taking off his sneakers. "I'd like to keep you company while we wait for her."

"That was thoughtful." Susie watched him as he pulled his socks off and rolled his jeans up, the way she had a few minutes earlier. "Did Taylor tell you about Izzy?"

"She said Izzy's the only one from that cast who's still alive. Did you get to meet her?"

"Yes. And she had nothing but great things to say about my mother."

"Sounds good."

Susie nodded as Kyle slipped his feet into the water next to hers.

"There was one odd thing. It turns out the woman Phil wants us to meet is Izzy and Olivia's daughter."

"Oh?"

"Olivia birthed her. I don't know if Izzy officially adopted her or just assumed the role of another mother."

Kyle touched Susie's foot with his own. Susie inched closer to him as he put his arm around her. Any remaining thoughts of Danny faded away. Kyle's touch felt warm, even his foot under the cool water. It was good she was free to feel nice around him. She leaned her head against Kyle's shoulder, resting her body against his while feeling the ripples on the surface of the lake against her ankles.

Susie breathed out slowly and spoke softly. "Nancy was my mother and Scott was my father. Maybe there's somebody else out there, somebody Phil or this woman BB knows about, but that won't change anything. Yet, I won't be satisfied we've learned all I need to know until I have the other shoe in my hand."

Kyle didn't respond to Susie's comment and, in the silence that followed, her thoughts drifted to those years she had spent on Halsey Island as a girl, waiting to see her best buddy Kyle who was always full of light.

She remembered walking through the woods with him, collecting large fungi that grew on fallen trees. They would scratch those plantlike objects, revealing a brown color underneath the smooth, white surface. They would draw pictures of the lake, the trees, the birds, and each other. Kyle would always find the most enormous fungus but she would draw the prettiest pictures.

She also remembered a time when she and Kyle had been sitting on the dock belonging to one of her family's island neighbors. They had hiked across the island and discovered a house she had only seen from the lake. No one appeared to be home, so Susie and Kyle had walked to the dock, a small pier. They were looking at the lake from a place with a very different view than the one from her own dock.

They heard something moving under them. Kyle wanted to leave but Susie refused. She went to the edge of the dock, got on her belly, and leaned way over to see underneath, her blond hair falling down into the water. This dock was built on a pile of rocks and raccoons were living among those stones. Susie saw a mother with two cubs. The large raccoon was on her side, nursing the two little ones. Susie could see fear in the animal's eyes but there was no way for them to escape.

"We have to leave," Susie said as she stood.

"Why?"

"There's a family of raccoons under here."

"Let me see!"

"You'll scare them. You don't want to do that."

Kyle looked anyway, but he was quiet and didn't frighten the animals. They left them alone after he had a good long look.

They were probably six years old when they discovered that raccoon den. Susie couldn't remember for sure. She wondered what it would have been like if they had spent that much time together when they were a little older, teenagers understanding their sexuality. Would desire have made much of a difference? As it was, they never thought of each other in sexual terms. There was that one time when they snuck into the boathouse and took off their clothes, but that wasn't anything more than curiosity.

Now here she was wondering about her life. She was drawn to Kyle. She didn't want to hurt Taylor, but they didn't act as if they were happy together, at least not exclusively together. Fact was, Kyle and Taylor both flirted with her. Susie also wondered about Danny.

Had she been fair to him, the man in her rearview mirror? Of course not. Yet it was good she'd ended it with him.

Susie had learned so much about her mother. Nancy had consoled people who had lovers in their lives the rest of society wouldn't accept back then. What would she have said about the complicated feelings Susie was experiencing now? Would she have encouraged them? Susie didn't think so. She would have wanted Susie to ignore what others say is right or wrong but also to do everything in her power not to hurt the surrounding people. That can be hard to do.

While Susie drifted through the thoughts of her past, she heard the flapping of sandals. Kyle must have heard the same sound because they jumped up and turned, moving together like Ginger dancing with Fred. Taylor was on the dock, walking toward them.

Taylor smiled and nodded. "You two ready to go?"

"Yep," Kyle told her, "Just waiting for you."

The Chris-Craft's slip was two back toward the shore. Kyle and Susie picked up their shoes and socks and tossed them in the boat. They untied and got in. Kyle backed away from the dock and headed under Brady Bridge toward Halsey Island. They didn't speak to each other as they crossed the lake. This was normal since they would have to shout over the engine but Taylor had seemed a little quieter than normal when she first walked out on the pier.

Susie worried that Taylor might have seen her snuggling with Kyle but when they reached the island both Kyle and Taylor acted as if nothing had happened. Taylor had some cooked salmon patties in the refrigerator. She heated them in the microwave, prepared a couple of servings of instant rice, and boiled a package of frozen spinach. After dinner, Susie cleared the table, then watched as Taylor and Kyle washed and dried the dishes. While they worked they listened to a Norah Jones album.

When the cleanup was done, Taylor turned to Susie and asked, "Would you like to take a sauna? It's a perfect night for one."

Susie's eyes bulged. "How?"

Kyle laughed. "We added one a couple of years ago. It's in the back of the boathouse. It's electric, so no smoke and all we have to do is flip a switch."

"Sounds wonderful but I don't have a bathing suit."

"You can wear one of mine," Taylor told her.

"I doubt any of yours would fit me."

"You can use the bottom from one of my two-piece suits and I have a t-shirt you can wear in place of the top."

The suggestion made sense. They both had small hips.

Susie agreed. Ten minutes later she was standing in front of a full-length mirror, upstairs in the lakeside bedroom, wearing a red and white striped bikini bottom with tie strings on both sides. The ties made it adjustable enough to fit perfectly. Taylor had given her a white shirt with blue letters saying *Fairleigh Dickinson University Alumni*. It was baggy but Susie was comfortable in it, although the red, white, and blue colors made her feel as if she was dressed in a flag.

The bikini bottom had less material than any other two-piece she'd ever worn. It wasn't much more than a thong. Her hips were exposed and a lot of her butt. The thin t-shirt covered the bottom, but it was white. Other than the blue letters it would cling to her skin and be transparent once she got in the water. She could picture herself, essentially topless, sitting across from Kyle and Taylor in their sauna. She wondered if Taylor had done this intentionally.

Taylor and Kyle were in a relationship, yet they both had dropped hints about wanting something with Susie, something more than friendship. Maybe they had an open relationship? That's the only way Susie could make any sense out of this and she didn't want to be part of something that complicated.

She pulled the t-shirt off, undid the bathing suit bottom, and got back into her clothes. When she stepped out into the hall, Taylor and Kyle were standing there, staring at her with confused looks.

"Aren't you coming with us?" Taylor asked.

"I changed my mind."

Kyle shook his head. "Oh, come on. It'll be fun."

"Have you ever taken a sauna?" Taylor asked her.

"Twice. I'm just not in the mood today. I've got so much to think about after talking to Izzy. You two go. I'll sit here and think."

Taylor sighed. "Suit yourself."

Kyle said, "If you want a glass of wine to sip on while you're thinking, there's an open bottle of a red blend on the kitchen counter and there are wine glasses in the cupboard."

Kyle and Taylor went downstairs and Susie followed. When they stepped onto the porch Susie went to the settee to watch them. It was twilight, so the footing wasn't as clear as it might have been in broad daylight. They were holding hands, maybe to keep their balance on the stone steps, or maybe just because they enjoyed holding hands. Both of them were walking with their heads held high and their shoulders back. They were having fun. Susie's stomach hardened. She didn't want them to have fun without her but what could she do?

She stood, ran inside, and up the stairs. She went back to the room where she had left the bathing suit Taylor had let her borrow. Susie changed again, putting on the suit bottom, then the bikini top, and finally the t-shirt. Her boobs were swimming in Taylor's top but with the shirt, she didn't look too foolish and the see-through white material was less of a problem.

Susie headed out of the bedroom, stopping at the bathroom to grab a towel, then went downstairs and out the front door. It was cool, and she had bare feet. The flat slates in the path felt like ice. It was also getting dark. She couldn't see the loose pebbles and protruding tree roots. Those could hurt but she made her way down to the boathouse. She took her time opening the door and closed it as quietly as she could. She had disappointed Taylor and Kyle when she turned down their invitation. Now she'd changed her mind and wanted to surprise them.

When Susie reached the sauna door, she could hear Taylor and Kyle talking on the other side of the wood door. She thought they might be discussing her but when Susie focused on their words, she discovered it was her mother they were talking about. She hadn't expected this.

"What else do you want to know about her?" Kyle's voice softened but Susie could still understand what he was asking.

"You knew her for a long time. You were thirteen when you last saw her, right? I'm wondering if you remember anything unusual. Nancy sounds as if she was a wonderful woman. She was open in her acceptance of gay people before the rest of society was.

Last Summer at Bluefish Cove must have been a controversial play when it was first produced. She was brave to accept the role of Eva."

"Brave?"

"Yes, she was. Do you remember anything else about her that seemed brave?"

Kyle paused before answering. "There was the time I fell out of the Chris-Craft." Susie pressed her ear against the door. She remembered when that happened and wanted to hear what Kyle had to say about it.

"I was leaning over the side of the boat. Susie's dad didn't have the boat at full throttle but it was still too fast for me. He hit a wave that rocked us and I went in. Nancy jumped out of the boat even before Scott slowed down. She swam to me and…"

Taylor interrupted. "She saved your life?"

"I wouldn't say that. I was scared, but I had a preserver on so I was floating on the surface. Still, Nancy reacted quickly, and that was brave."

"I was looking for something else." Taylor's voice faded as if she was thinking of the right words to use. "Emotionally brave is what I'm talking about. Do you remember ever seeing her in a situation that called for her to be under control while her emotions were flailing about like hurricane winds?"

"There was that one time," Kyle said, speaking slowly again, "when her husband died. I wasn't there but I know about it. Susie told me everything her mother went through."

Chapter Twenty-Four

Eleven Years Earlier

Susie was at the kitchen table, slurping spoonfuls of minestrone soup between bites of a toasted cheese sandwich. It was a Saturday afternoon. Nancy was washing the frying pan she'd used to cook the sandwich. There was a rumble, a series of pops and cracks, then a loud crunch. The sound came from outside the house. Nancy ran past Susie who was frozen in place, her spoon halfway to her mouth. She darted around the kitchen table and out the back door.

A second later she screamed. A huge Ash tree had fallen and was lying on the ground. Her husband was underneath it. Scott had told Susie and Nancy to stay indoors until the tree was on the ground but he hadn't worried about his own safety. This was not the first large tree he'd taken down. It was, however, the first one that had fallen wrong.

Nancy could see the angled slot in the stump that was supposed to direct the fall. Maybe the land had more of a slope than Scott had considered. Maybe the tree's branches were too heavy on the side toward him. Whatever it was, Scott's bloody body was underneath a twisted mat of hardwood branches.

His head had split open as if a meat cleaver had hit him. Another branch was sticking out of his chest, filled with blood that must have spurted up like a geyser before his heart stopped. There was no doubt he was dead but Nancy moved forward anyway, diving into the twisted mat of leaves and sticks like a rabbit running to hide.

She shoved and pulled at the small branches and climbed over the large ones. The t-shirt and shorts she was wearing offered no protection which meant her face, neck, arms, legs, and even her belly were getting cut up as if she was walking through a paper shredder. She almost lost an eye to branches that swung at her. Yet she persisted and finally reached Scott. She wrapped her arms around him as best she could, letting his blood soak into her ripped clothes and skin. She kissed him, cried over him, and prayed for him. Then, because there was nothing else she could do, she went back to find Susie and call for help.

Susie was no longer in the kitchen. She was upstairs in her room, looking out her window at the tragedy in the backyard. Susie had vomited over herself, the floor, and the wall beneath the window. She was thirteen now and hated when her mother treated her like a child but this horrible tragedy made everything different. Susie was in shock and needed comfort.

Using tissues from a box on Susie's desk, Nancy wiped her husband's blood off her own face and clothing then cleaned up her daughter. Ignoring the rest of the mess, she took her girl in her arms and rocked her. Nancy sang *O Danny Boy* and *The Bonnie Banks o' Loch Lomond*, tunes she had sung to Susie when she was a young child. The phone call could wait. Scott was dead and no one could do anything about that now.

She finally made the call after comforting Susie for over an hour. Nancy explained the situation to the woman who answered the phone at police headquarters. "This is more complicated than simply sending an ambulance. We're on an island in Lake Hopatcong. I'm certain my husband died as soon as..." Her voice was shaking. "...as soon as the tree fell but I need help. The longer he lies there, the more this will affect our daughter." She took a breath. "Please send an ambulance quickly along with a couple of men. And have the men bring chainsaws. I can meet you somewhere in my boat."

"No need for that. You stay with your daughter. The Marine Police can get our officers to you. Tell me which island."

"Halsey—I'm sorry. I can hardly speak."

"That's all right. Take a breath and tell me your name and which side of the island you're on."

"The southern side. I'm Nancy Walsh. My husband is Scott Walsh...or was Scott." She felt dizzy and held on to Susie's bureau to keep from falling over. "I'm trying to keep it together and it's hard."

"We'll find you. Don't worry. You're doing great."

Nancy gripped her throat. "My daughter and I can go to the dock to wait for you. We'll signal when we see your boat."

"Good. We'll have an ambulance waiting by the Marine Headquarters. You just take care of your daughter and yourself."

"Don't forget the chainsaws. There are so many branches."

Nancy hung up the phone then put her arm around Susie. They helped each other walk downstairs and out of the house. When they reached the dock, Susie sat on one of the dock chairs while Nancy stood, keeping watch for the Marine Police. If it had been summer instead of fall, one of her neighbors might have offered to wait with them but the few other families who came to the island off-season all lived on the other side.

When the boat arrived, they tied up along the side of the dock. There were five men aboard, two Jefferson police officers, two paramedics with a large bag of medical equipment and a stretcher, and a single state police officer, who drove the boat.

"Where was the accident?" one officer asked.

Nancy took a step forward then stopped. "Around back." She clenched her hands. "I can show you. Can someone stay here with Susie? I don't want her to see him like this again."

"I'm all right," Susie said but all the color had drained from her face and her chin was trembling.

"I'll stay with her," the state police officer offered. "And you need to take care of those cuts on your face and arms."

"I'm OK, but thank you." Nancy released a breath and started walking off the dock.

After she showed the men where Scott's body was, she went back to Susie and took her to the house. They sat in the living room, in silence, as they listened to the chainsaws. Nancy couldn't find the right words to say to her daughter so they used the silence as a time to pray. Nancy prayed for Scott, for Susie, and for herself. Although there were still streaks from the tears that had flowed down Susie's cheeks, she was no longer crying. Nancy didn't know if that was a good thing. Susie seemed too still, almost catatonic.

A police officer came into the living room quietly, his shoulders shaking. "They've freed his body and are taking it to the boat, Ma'am. We have to go now. Is there anyone who can sit with you?"

Nancy shook her head. She stood up but kept her eyes on Susie.

The officer pulled a card from his shirt pocket. "Do you have a pen?"

Nancy grabbed one from the table beside the piano and handed it to him.

"This is the number of my church. If you need to talk to someone and you don't know anyone else to call, then call this number. The church secretary is a wonderful woman. She'll talk to you as long as you need her or pass you on to our minister."

"Thank you."

"Is there anything else I can do for you?"

There wasn't. Nancy went to the front window and watched as that officer walked down to the dock. He was alone. They had already carried Scott's body down. She watched as he got into the boat with the others, then rode away with what was left of the man she loved.

Scott and Nancy hadn't discussed what to do if one of them died unexpectedly so she hadn't chosen a funeral home. The officer told her they would take the body to the county morgue in Morristown. That was fine with her. It would give her time to think of how to honor him. He would always be the love of her life.

"Would you like a coke?" Nancy asked her daughter.

Susie shrugged.

"I need something a little stronger so I'm going to have a glass of wine. You can have one also if you want to. This has been a horrible day. I can't imagine anything worse. A glass of wine might ease the pain."

Susie shook her head. "I don't…" Her voice faded out but Nancy knew what she meant. Susie's father was gone. The pain of losing him was all she had left.

"I'll get cokes for both of us."

Nancy looked out the kitchen window as she poured the sodas. The men had cut branches out of the way to free Scott's body but they hadn't removed the tree. She would have to call someone else to deal with that.

It took more than a month to get the area around the house cleared. Nancy used that time to think things through. Scott had been the breadwinner in their family. Now she was a single mother with no money-making skills. Scott had often said there was only one economic rule that counted. You need to spend less than you make. If she was going to follow that advice she had to do two things. She needed to cut expenses and make a decent income. She decided to sell the island and mainland homes, find an inexpensive place to live, and take a course to learn a trade.

She enrolled in the Dental Hygienist course at Raritan Valley Community College. She and Susie lived off the money from Scott's insurance and the sale of the two homes until Nancy could land a decent job. The job turned out to be a blessing in two ways. She could provide for her small family and, when Susie graduated from high school, Nancy recommended her daughter to be the office receptionist.

Chapter Twenty-Five

2022

Susie didn't want to risk getting caught eavesdropping which meant she had to get out of the boathouse before Kyle and Taylor discovered her. They'd been in the sauna for quite a while and his story had ended. They could come out for a dip in the lake any minute. She tiptoed to the outside door, opened it gently, and closed it behind her. She darted up the hill but off to the side, by the forest, rather than staying on the path, to avoid being seen from the dock. Once she was inside, she changed back into her street clothes. She went downstairs and poured a glass of the wine Kyle had mentioned. She went out on the porch and watched the dock.

Taylor and Kyle were in the water now. They swam from the front of the dock to the shallow area, walked back to the steps to get out of the lake, and dove in again. They both repeated this ritual twice, then got out, kissed, and entered the boathouse.

After a few times in the sauna, they headed up the path, carrying their towels and holding hands with each other. Taylor was grinning when she and Kyle reached Susie. "You missed a good time. The water was perfect, chilly enough to whip us a bit when we first jumped in. After that, it felt like nirvana. We went back three times."

"I know. I was watching."

"You stay right there," Kyle told Susie. "We'll change out of our suits and be back in a flash." He put his chilly hand on her shoulder. Even though it was cold, she liked the way his touch felt. "I'll open another bottle of that red blend. It's nice, isn't it?"

Susie nodded while Taylor smiled and tugged on Kyle's other hand.

When they returned, Kyle was wearing a pair of dark blue running shorts and a light blue t-shirt. He had the open bottle he'd promised in his hand.

Taylor had on a thin, white robe. Poking out from underneath, Susie could see enough yellow to know she was wearing the sexy nightgown Susie had seen in the wardrobe.

The knowledge of what that gown meant to them made Susie uncomfortable at first. She glanced at Kyle expecting he would be uncomfortable as well, but he didn't seem to be affected by that or anything else, just interested in his glass of red wine. She raised her eyebrows, shook her head, and took another sip of hers.

They had spent a good deal of time in the sauna so it wasn't long before they were ready for bed. Taylor and Susie were planning to meet BB the following day while Kyle worked. They all had to be rested.

Susie did not want to sleep in her street clothes because this meeting with BB was important. She wanted to feel as fresh as she could, given she hadn't brought a change of clothes with her. She put on the white t-shirt Taylor had given her for the sauna, laid out her clothes, and went to bed.

Susie lay there until she heard the sounds of sex, once again coming from Kyle and Taylor's room. It made her feel lonely. She decided she would take the sauna they'd offered earlier, even though she'd be alone. Susie got up, sneaked out of the house, and went down to the boathouse. She went inside, straight to the door of the sauna. There were two switches on the side wall near a temperature gauge. One was the light switch. The other had to be the way to turn on the heat. She flipped it and quickly felt warmth from the heater.

Susie pulled off the t-shirt she was wearing. She didn't want it to get wet when she jumped in the lake. She was alone and there were few boats on the water. No one would notice she was naked.

The heat was meditative, so much she had to be careful she didn't fall asleep. She thought of Kyle and Taylor. They were so conservative on the outside, a human resource manager and an accountant, of all things. But they had their wild sides.

Kyle's personality had changed little since they were young. He was still gentle, still caring, still kind. Taylor was the same, and she was the one most interested in finding Ginger's shoe. They were right for each other and she would not get in their way.

When the sauna had worked its magic and Susie needed to wash the sweat off her skin, she left the sauna and the boathouse. The cool air felt wonderful against her bare skin but she needed to get in the water before she cooled off too much. She followed the same path Taylor and Kyle had followed earlier, running to the edge of the dock, diving in, then swimming to the shallow and walking through the water to the steps.

Susie decided one swim in the lake was enough. She needed a decent night's rest to be alert for the meeting with BB the next day. She went back into the boathouse to turn off the sauna heater and the lights. Susie was soaking wet and didn't want to get her t-shirt wet. She carried it rather than put it on.

Susie moved up the path, across the porch, and slipped into the front door as quietly as she could, going directly to the stairs, then down the hall toward her bedroom. She turned quickly when she felt someone watching, but no one was there. She was being paranoid.

Susie was dry except for her hair by the time she was in her room. She slipped on the t-shirt and moved toward the bed. It was then she noticed someone in the doorway. The room was dark, but the moonlight lit the room enough for Susie to see. It was Taylor.

"You went for a swim?"

"I couldn't sleep." Susie wondered how long Taylor had been standing there. "I took a sauna. I hope that's okay. It relaxed me."

"That's fine. You turned off the heater, right?" Susie nodded and Taylor said, "Good."

Taylor left the room and closed the door. Susie went to bed but now the notion that Taylor had been watching her, filled her mind. It took her a few minutes to fall asleep.

The following morning, Susie dressed in the clothes she'd been wearing when Taylor met her outside the office. She went downstairs to find Taylor and Kyle already up. Kyle had made scrambled eggs and bacon. Susie skipped the bacon but enjoyed the eggs and toast.

Neither Taylor nor Kyle said anything about her late-night sauna. Susie was happy Taylor wasn't making an issue of it and hoped she had mentioned nothing to Kyle.

Taylor planned to go with Susie to BB's apartment around 10:00. Hopefully, she would be home and willing to talk. Even though it was a Saturday, Kyle needed to be at work. Taylor had to give him a ride to Bridge Marina, then bring the Chris-Craft back so she and Susie could get off the island later.

When Taylor and Kyle were ready to go, Susie moved to the porch where she could sip on her second cup of coffee and munch on a cinnamon roll. She watched as they left their dock and waited until she could see Taylor coming back. This gave her time to think.

Susie had a feeling she was getting closer to the answer she was looking for. Perhaps BB had the shoe but even if she didn't Susie had already discovered things about her mother, she'd never known. She now realized Nancy had treated people outside her family with kindness and offered advice with common sense. That was the way her mother had always dealt with Susie, even when Susie didn't realize she needed help. But perhaps there was something else, something even more significant. Hopefully, BB would help them find all the answers. Both Phil Robinson and Izzy Evans had given BB's name to her. She had to be important.

Although the sky was cloudy and the ozone-rich scent in the air was a sure sign of impending rain, Taylor got Kyle to Bridge Marina and the boat back before the storm started. Shortly after she pulled into the boathouse, it poured. She held a lifejacket over her head as she ran up the hill. It provided little cover, so she was drenched when she reached the porch.

Taylor laughed, then shook like a dog. "Wait here. I have to change." She dropped the wet lifejacket and went through the door. Susie took another sip of her coffee. It was lukewarm, but she was too comfortable to go inside to heat it.

When Taylor returned she was wearing jeans and a red, long-sleeved t-shirt. "I've got a change of clothes in here." She lifted a small suitcase she was carrying. "We'll wait for the rain to stop but I'll still have to cover the boat at the dock. I don't want to get dirty doing that. When I'm done, I'll change in the ladies' room. I brought ponchos for both of us, in case the rain starts again but I don't think it will. The sky is clearing."

Susie was still wearing the clothes she had put on for work the previous day. Her outfit would be fine for dropping in on BB but she didn't know about Taylor. She hoped the dress that Taylor had put in the tiny suitcase would be all right for visiting someone neither of them knew.

The ride to Bridge Marina stayed dry. They rode in silence because the engine noise and the ponchos they were wearing made a conversation difficult to hear. Once they arrived, Susie waited inside the marina while Taylor covered the Chris-Craft, then for a few minutes longer while she changed her clothes.

When Taylor came out, the dress she'd chosen pleased Susie. Taylor was in a green, sleeveless dress with a skirt that reached knee height. The dress had pleats on the shoulders and the skirt. The material had a blue floral pattern. It was a nice match for what Susie was wearing.

Once they were in Susie's car, driving toward BB's home, they could talk.

The conversation began with an unexpected touch. Taylor put her hand on Susie's arm. Susie was not used to anyone touching her while she was driving. She wrenched her arm away from Taylor. The car swerved but Susie got it back under control. They were lucky no one was driving in the lane next to theirs when that happened.

"Sorry," Taylor said in a low voice.

Susie glanced at her and noticed Taylor was holding her hands up.

"Please, don't touch me when I'm driving."

"It won't happen again. I just wanted your attention."

"You've got that but I have to keep my eyes on the road.'

"Of course." Taylor cleared her throat. "Thank you for letting me be a part of this search of yours."

"I'm the one who should thank you. Your research has helped and discovering Izzy was wonderful. She taught me so much about my mother."

"I'm glad but what you did for me is more. This search of yours introduced me to your mother. I have respect for the women who were part of the early productions of *Last Summer at Bluefish Cove*. Your mother played the most important role in the show and then played a role in the lives of the friends she made, friends who were suffering from the homophobic prejudices so prevalent in the twentieth century."

Susie was convinced Taylor was attracted to her. She was certain Taylor's admiration for Nancy had to be connected to Taylor's own sexuality. But was that bad? Her mother wouldn't have thought so.

Susie could hear Taylor taking in a deep breath, then releasing it slowly. Then Taylor said, "I think the bravest people are not the ones who are threatened, but the ones who stand up for others. Think of Schindler's List. What did that man have to gain by saving all those people? He wasn't Jewish."

"I don't think you can equate the risk my mother took with the risk Schindler took."

"True. But that's just a question of degree. I admire your mother as much as I admire anyone else who stands up for what's right."

"What about you? Have you been one of those people who steps forward for a cause that doesn't directly affect you?"

"I haven't."

"So tell me why you admire my mom so much but have done nothing like that yourself."

Taylor shook her head softly. "It's a matter of strength."

"And motivation, I would think." Susie gripped the steering wheel harder.

"Maybe you're right. Sometimes I just want to have fun."

"Nothing wrong with that but fun can't be all your life, can it?"

Taylor winced. "It shouldn't be."

They were both silent for a while. Finally, Taylor spoke, saying, "I get out of my comfort zone in ways that are fun but can also hurt."

"Really? Like what?" Susie glanced at Taylor and saw her eyes were closed.

Taylor let out a short, little laugh then said, "For one thing, I believe I'm falling in love with someone Kyle loves. That's a brave thing to do, isn't it?"

They drove on in silence for the additional twenty minutes it took to get to BB's apartment. Susie wasn't upset. She just didn't know what to say and there was Kyle to think about. Both of them, Taylor in particular, had been so understanding and helpful with her mother's last request. This situation was too strange. Taylor's declaration felt real and Susie could not return it. Still, she had never imagined she could even think about a relationship with a woman. That was a step but was it forward or backward?

Chapter Twenty-Six

They parked on Claremont Avenue in the closest space they could find, then walked up a sloped walkway, through the main doors, and into a large, marble-lined entranceway leading up a set of stairs to an inside, glass door. They tried that door and found it locked. There was a panel of doorbell buttons on the wall to the right of the door. Brooke Bevans's name was next to one of those. Susie rang the bell.

In less than a minute, a woman's voice came through the speaker. "Hello. Who's there?"

"We're looking for BB."

"That's me. Who are you?"

"Izzy Evans sent us."

"My mother?"

"Yes. Can you buzz us in?"

"Wait there. I want to see you first."

"All right."

"I'll be right down."

Taylor stood about ten feet behind Susie as they looked through the glass door and waited for BB to show. In a couple of minutes, they saw a blond woman coming down the stairs and heading their way. When she reached the entrance she looked at Susie, then at Taylor, and only then did she partially open the door. The woman was younger than Susie by about five years if Susie's guess was right. Her hair was close to the color of Susie's and cut in a similar style. She was a couple of inches shorter and a little heavier, but the most exciting similarity was her eyes. This woman had crystal-blue eyes just like Susie's!

Susie reached up and pulled off her sunglasses. The woman gasped, "Susie!"

"Yes. That's my name. How did you know?"

"I know about you even though you don't know me. I saw you as Lily in *The Secret Garden*. My mother, Olivia, gave me the tickets and disguised me so you wouldn't notice how much we look alike. She bought me a cheap wig and tinted glasses. It was fun. I've waited for years to meet you!"

"What do you mean?"

"We're sisters." BB looked at Taylor, then back at Susie. "You and your friend need to come in. I'll explain."

Chapter Twenty-Seven

Twenty-Seven Years Earlier

Nancy met Phil Robinson at The Jefferson House. It was two o'clock on a sunny Saturday afternoon in September. There were a few other customers but Phil and Nancy were the only ones on the patio. It was off season. Phil wasn't sure there would be service where they were so he got their drinks. He was back now and Nancy was sipping on a White Russian while Phil was enjoying a J&B on the rocks.

There were sailboats on the lake, racing in a regatta the yacht club sponsored. Susie didn't know what type of sailboats they were but they were fun to watch as each boat tried to juggle for position and make the most of the limited breeze. There were a few motorboats in the main section of the lake mingling with them, trying to stay out of their way.

"I have something to tell you," Phil said, leaning forward with a wide grin. "I found a surrogate."

"That's great news." Nancy felt her pulse jump. "What's her background?"

"She's an actress."

Phil went quiet so Nancy asked, "Is that all you're going to tell me?"

"What do you want to know?"

"Well...her ethnicity for one thing."

"Her family name is Bennett. I believe that's an English surname."

"Bennett? I know someone named Bennett, someone who's also an actress."

"I know you do. Let me explain. When I saw you were involved with the show *Last Summer at Bluefish Cove,* I approached the cast. It's a liberal play. I thought they might be amiable to the request."

Nancy felt her core go cold. "You're saying you recruited Olivia Bennett to be my surrogate?"

"Only if you accept her."

"I could have asked her myself but I didn't because she's a friend of mine."

"I know you *could* have but you *wouldn't* have. You know that's true." He let out a breath slowly. "Think about it. Olivia will bear a child for you, a child who'll be a mix of Scott and someone you love and respect. You can't have your own child so this is the best you can do. That's got to be worth the money you paid me."

Nancy felt her eyes water. She shook her head. "I hear you and I agree Olivia is a wonderful woman. But I thought I would deal with a stranger for nine months, then never see her again."

"It's longer than nine. There's the period of trying until the woman's pregnant. That can take a while."

"You know what I mean. I didn't think it would be someone I know, someone who will still be a friend as I raise my child."

"What you do after the baby is born is up to you. You can stay in touch with Olivia or the two of you can go your separate ways."

"I love my friendship with Olivia and Izzy. I don't want to give that up."

"Again. Up to you."

There was another pause before Nancy said, "I can't tell you yes, not today. I have to see Olivia. I need to look into her eyes and understand what she's thinking. She doesn't need the money, so this is not one of the starving actresses you deal with in your business. Why is she agreeing to this? I think she's doing it as an act of love for me and I'm not sure I want that complication in this process."

Nancy met Olivia at Monte's Trattoria in Greenwich Village. It was a lovely Italian restaurant with plenty of tables for two where they could have a private conversation. Nancy and Olivia had both eaten there previously, although never together. They started by sharing a bottle of Merlot before they discussed anything related to surrogacy. They talked about Olivia's relationship with Izzy. Things were still going well for them and Nancy expressed her joy in that fact.

After the waiter took their orders Olivia brought up the reason they were there. "When Phil Robinson approached me I was shocked. I never thought of serving as a surrogate. I had thought of artificial insemination because I want a child of my own someday, but I never considered birthing a child for someone else. When he mentioned you were the one reaching out, I gave more thought to this possibility. I love the things you did for me and Izzy. You have always been a great friend."

"That's what I fear. I didn't ask Phil to approach you. He's the one who suggested I might want someone I know rather than some anonymous woman, someone I respect and admire. I understood his point, but there are so many complications. I don't want my child's birth mother in the picture. I want my baby to think of me as her mother, her only mother. And I don't want any interference in the decisions I make."

"I can be as distant as you want me to be."

Nancy shrugged.

"When Phil approached me, and I got over my initial surprise, the proposal flattered me. I thought you wanted me because you thought of me as the best choice since you can't have your own baby." Olivia rolled her eyes. "I'm stumbling over what I'm trying to say." She took a breath. "I thought you respected my attitude about life and wanted a child capable of having that same attitude."

"I do. It isn't the woman you are that makes me hesitate. It's our friendship."

"You won't lose my friendship. Even if you decide to break off all contact with me while you raise your daughter I will still be your friend. Anytime you choose to reach out I will be there because you've been there when I needed you the most." She reached across the table and grabbed Nancy's hand. "I want you to understand that, but there's something else that might make you hesitate." She let go of Nancy's hand and took a drink of her wine. "I want to birth your child. I also want to have a child of my own. We're not ready yet. I feel too young and Izzy is younger than me. Scott is a wonderful man. I believe a daughter or son with a mixture of his genes and mine would be the child you would want and also, the child I want."

"I don't understand what you're saying."

"I'm saying I don't want money for doing this. Whatever you decide, I'll return my portion of what you gave Phil. Instead, I want something else. Besides birthing your child, I want to put some of Scott's sperm in storage. A few years from now, when Izzy and I are ready, I want to birth a second child, a full sibling of yours. I know this is a shock and if you don't agree with what I want to do, I'll still give birth to your child. But I think it would be wonderful for us to have children that might eventually know each other. We could keep them separate for as long as you wish. But this arrangement could be the answer to both our prayers. Please think about what I'm suggesting."

"I'll talk it over with Scott. I'm not sure how he'll feel. Would he be able to know your child? If so, how will I be able to keep my secret?"

"All that can work out. And, just like you, I don't want anyone interfering with the way I choose to raise the son or daughter I have."

Chapter Twenty-Eight

"Was I adopted?" BB's youthful voice was uncertain.

Olivia sat on the couch beside her daughter and reached for her hand. "Where did you hear such a thing?"

"Aaron said I was." BB was always bringing home something from kindergarten for her moms to deal with. Sometimes it was a cold, or a bruised knee but this time it was a tricky question. "He said you have to be adopted if you have two moms."

"He said that?"

BB nodded.

"Well…Aaron is only partially right."

"His daddy told him I had to be adopted because I don't have a daddy."

Olivia sighed. "Did he? Do you understand what adopted is?"

"No. But Aaron made it sound bad."

"It's not bad. It's very good. Most adoptions happen when a woman has a baby but knows she can't take care of her or him. There can be many reasons but when that happens the best thing to do is to find other people who want a child to love. That person or people will take care of the baby and give her or him a good life. But that's not what happened to you, not exactly. You were adopted but only by Little Mommy."

Izzy entered the room from the kitchen and interrupted. "I heard what you two are talking about." She looked at Olivia. "May I tell this part?"

Olivia nodded.

Izzy sat on the floor in front of the couch and leaned toward BB. "You're in a big girl school now. You're old enough to understand things we couldn't tell you before." Izzy blew out her cheeks. "Big Mommy and I are two women in a marriage that works because we love each other and because we both love you. That's what's important for any family." She touched BB's nose. "We could not have a child without the help of a man. That's true. There are ways to get help by going to a doctor and we talked about doing that." Izzy smiled and lowered her voice. "Then an odd situation came along and we discovered a way we could get help from someone we knew and respected. After that, you grew inside Big Mommy for nine months and, when the time was right, you were born. I loved you as much as anyone can love a child, so I adopted you."

"Which is why you have two mommies," Olivia told BB, "and that's a good thing, a wonderful thing."

Olivia and Izzy were both actresses, which meant their work schedules did not coincide with BB's school hours. Yet there was always someone home in the evening to make dinner, help BB with her homework, and do whatever other parental tasks were required. They told BB they tried to arrange their projects so when Big Mommy had a role, Izzy was home and when Izzy was rehearsing for a show, Olivia was home but sometimes Olivia's mother had to be called in to help.

Evelyn was in her sixties but an active woman who loved to take BB outside to play a game of catch or go bike riding with her. She's the person who started playing tennis with BB when she was seven, a sport BB loved from the start.

Chapter Twenty-Nine

With two actresses for her mothers, BB was in plenty of pageants and plays during her elementary school days and took voice lessons starting in sixth grade. However, when she was about to enter high school, she made an announcement. "I am going to make the tennis team in my freshman year." This, of course, meant she would have little time for school plays.

BB had been attending high school for just a week when Olivia and Izzy asked her to come to the kitchen table. BB was calling them by their first names now that she was in ninth grade.

Izzy pressed her lips together, then spoke. "We have something we need to discuss with you."

"Yes," Olivia interrupted, looking into BB's eyes. "We think you're old enough to understand."

"Your biological father died when you were young," Izzy told BB. "There was never a possibility you could meet him. But you have a sister who is alive and doing well. Olivia is her birth mother, as well as yours, and you both had the same father. But her mother, the woman who raised her, requested we stay out of her life."

"Why?"

"She didn't want confusion."

"Confusion?"

"Yes, about which woman was her mother." Olivia bit her lip as Izzy continued to speak. "Situations like this can be confusing for a young child. That's why we waited until now to tell you. We didn't agree with her decision but it was her right to make it and we have honored her choice."

"Your sister is eighteen," Olivia told her. "We still don't want to go against her mother's wishes but if we get caught now, it'll be easier to explain."

"You're taking me to meet her?"

"No, not to meet her. But you will get to see her."

BB's eyes narrowed.

Olivia took a breath, then explained. "She's an actress, like us." Olivia smiled at Izzy. "She's in a play called *The Secret Garden*, playing a ghost named Lily. The show is in a theater in New Jersey and we've purchased tickets. This way you'll be able to see her without meeting her. Does this make sense?"

"Not really. What's her name?"

"Susie Walsh. You'll find that out when we see the show so we might as well tell you now." Olivia cleared her throat. "There's another problem. Susie and you look alike. You both have blond hair and crystal-blue eyes."

"You've seen her?"

"Yes, from a distance."

"But close enough to see her eyes?"

"Yes."

"We're going to disguise ourselves," Izzy told her. "Our plan is to get you tinted glasses and a wig. Olivia and I are also going to wear wigs. Susie Walsh would not recognize either of us but if her mom is there, *she* might."

The night of the show was amazing. Susie Walsh had a voice as smooth as ripples on a lake. She sang a duet called *How Could I Ever Know* and nailed every note. The man she was with had a nice voice but Susie's shivered up BB's spine. It was as if a sound she had always heard inside her soul had escaped and was now filling the entire room.

When the show was over, the cast came out and BB saw Susie up close. Now she knew for sure, Susie had the eyes BB had only seen in mirrors. Izzy grabbed BB's elbow and led her out of the theater before the sisters talked.

BB was quiet during the drive back but when they reached their home she said. "I don't know if this is the reason you did this with me now but, if so, it worked and I'm grateful. I will not play tennis in school. I'm going to concentrate all my efforts on singing, dancing, and acting. My goal is to be as good as my sister."

Chapter Thirty

2022

After BB finished telling Olivia and Nancy's story, she went quiet. Susie was also silent, too shocked to speak.

Susie was having trouble processing this bizarre information and trouble understanding the reasons her mother had kept her in the dark. Nancy's insecurity had kept them apart, which probably hurt BB the most since she knew what was happening. But Susie was still envious that BB had known of their relationship while she had known nothing. She was also angry. She had trusted her mother and Nancy hadn't deserved that trust. Susie had always thought of Nancy as strong and brave, but her silence was a coward's way of lying.

Although she was jealous of BB, it also thrilled her to have a sister. Today's revelation meant Susie and BB were a family. And, after losing her mother, Susie needed that connection.

Susie looked at BB and smiled, but it was Taylor who broke the silence. "Then you have the shoe?"

BB nodded, and they all laughed.

* * *

The following weekend, Taylor and Kyle threw a party at the Halsey Island house to celebrate the reuniting of Ginger's left and right shoes. They invited Susie of course but also Izzy and BB. They displayed the shoes on the coffee table in the living room.

The meal was salmon patties, spinach salad, and corn on the cob. It was late in the season for the corn but everything tasted good. The wine helped. Taylor opened two bottles: one Pinot Noir and another Cabernet Sauvignon.

After dinner, Kyle, Taylor, and Izzy cleaned the table while BB and Susie carried their glasses out to the porch. It was a Saturday afternoon, but the lake was relatively quiet since summer was over. There were five motor boats skimming across the water. Susie counted them. But there were no sailboats, no kayaks, and no skiers behind the motor boats. Some trees along the shore had turned yellow but not all of them. She couldn't find any red leaves at all. Still, the hills surrounding the lake looked pretty.

Susie took a deep breath. "I love this time of the season." She turned to BB and smiled. "When my family owned this house, my father used to bring us here on the weekends until the first freeze. We would set up a grill and cook hamburgers on the porch. Then Mom and Dad would relax and enjoy the beauty of everything. I was too young to appreciate what they were feeling, but I knew my parents loved each other by the way they could take in the wonders of this lake together. Looking back on that time, it seems as if they shared one soul."

"You're saying they were soul mates?"

Susie brought a finger to her cheek to catch a tear. "I guess so." She took in a breath, then continued, "And I could appreciate their connection even though I was young. I was thirteen when I lost him."

BB leaned toward Susie. "Can you tell me more about him?"

"About my father?"

"Yes. Olivia and Izzy were wonderful parents, but he was my birth father. I want to know more."

"There are plenty of stories to tell but this one I think you'll like." Susie's gaze softened for a moment then brightened as she focused on her memories. "My father taught me to swim. There's a shallow area on the other side of the island we called the sandbar. Every day, for a few weeks, he took me to that place in the rowboat. We would anchor close to shore where the water was calm. He would get out and stand, then lift me from the boat into the water, carefully holding me so I would feel secure. I remember how he positioned me with my back up, then placed his hand under my belly, and walked alongside me as I tried to swim. He taught me the doggy paddle, telling me to reach forward one arm at a time and to pull the water back toward me while I kicked my legs. He said to dip my head in the water to exhale but it scared me to do that so I kept my head up. I was moving forward but I couldn't tell how much was me swimming and how much was Dad guiding me through the water until he let go. There were many memories I've thought about after he passed but that is the one I keep going back to. There was something beautiful about the way he led me through the water until he didn't need to. I guess that's what parenting is about."

BB sighed and placed her hand on Susie's arm. "You're right. That's what it's about. My moms didn't teach me to swim. Instead, they sent me to the Y. But there were other moments where they showed their love."

"Tell me about those," Susie said, putting her hand over BB's.

"The closest memory I have to your father teaching you how to swim was when Izzy taught me to ride a bike. She ran next to me with her hand on the back of the seat until she didn't have to, the same way your father kept his hand on your stomach. Then one day I stopped, put my leg out so I wouldn't fall over, and turned around. She was way back across the parking lot, at least twenty yards behind me. It surprised me and shook me but I loved her for it."

"That's wonderful but tell me about Olivia. I want to learn about her for the same reasons you want to learn about my father."

"All right. Here's something. You know she was an actress right?" BB's eyes shone. "Well—she wanted me involved in theater, too. She signed me up for dance classes and I didn't like them. The theater bug didn't get to me until I saw you in *The Secret Garden,* even after Olivia talked a friend of hers into casting me as one of the Von Trapp children in a production of *The Sound of Music.* They ended up having to drop me from the cast because I had no enthusiasm. I showed up, but I was boring to watch." BB laughed. "I told Olivia I was interested in horseback riding. You'd expect she would have fought me on that because my interest was so different from hers and because she was scared of horses. But she did what a wonderful mom does. She found a horse farm in Chester."

"In Chester? That's the town where I perform."

"I know but let me finish."

Susie nodded.

"She would take me to the farm after school on Thursdays so I could take lessons and she even leased a horse for me. We competed in shows but we never did well. The horse I had wasn't very competitive, at least that's what Mom said. She offered to buy a horse since the ones available to lease were not the best but I knew how tight money was and how expensive horses can be. Besides, by the time she made the offer, I was more interested in boys. I always loved her for allowing me to be me and taking the time to support my interest.

"Olivia and Izzy filled in the spots that dads normally do and held up the spots that moms usually do. They were great with all of that but I always wonder about my birth father."

"I understand. I didn't wonder about my birth mother because I did not know I was adopted until recently. But now I know where I came from and I'd like to learn more about her."

"I have something that might help both of you." The voice came from the doorway to the house. They turned to see Izzy. She grinned while stepping toward them, holding a large, canvas shopping bag.

"Scott and Olivia knew each other. They would meet once a year to go shopping together, to help each other buy gifts for both of you. Olivia would buy something for Susie and Scott would buy something for BB. I knew about this arrangement but Nancy didn't. She was stubborn about keeping you, Susie, in the dark about the circumstances of your birth. She would have seen their annual get-together as a risk that might reveal her secret.

"They would buy small things but never pass them on to either of you. The purpose wasn't so you two would know them but so they would each learn something about the child they couldn't visit. They couldn't give the things they bought to you girls. That's why all the gifts are still in this bag." She nodded at the two women. "This secret shopping started happening on BB's first birthday." Izzy looked at Susie. "You were six. It ended when you were thirteen and BB was eight."

"When my father died, right?"

"Yes. Olivia couldn't do it on her own and your mother knew nothing about this. I never understood why it was so important to her that you continued to think she gave birth to you. She'd been a close friend to Olivia and me before you were born. After that, she wanted nothing to do with us but that's not important now." Izzy turned her attention back to the items in the shopping bag. "Let me show you what they bought."

Chapter Thirty-One

Olivia pulled out two small packages wrapped in white paper. S6 was written on one and B1 on the other. She handed them to the two women who quickly unwrapped them. BB's was a pad of paper and a crayon. Susie's was a plastic Kaleidoscope. They both held up their gifts and looked at each other with blank expressions.

Susie's eyes narrowed. "You've kept these since I was six?"

Izzy shrugged. "I've kept them since Olivia died. She kept them before that. She and Scott wouldn't give the gifts to either of you because Nancy didn't want you to know about your birth mother or your sister."

"Why?" BB asked, frowning. She had always wondered about Scott and Susie, but she'd given little thought to Nancy. Susie's mother was just an annoying, distant presence who had kept BB away from a part of her family.

Izzy paused. "I guess Nancy was insecure, although I didn't get that impression through anything else I knew about her. Some mothers worry their adopted children might dream of a different life with the woman who gave them up. I guess she was one of them."

"I loved life with my parents. I never dreamed of living with anyone else."

"Sometimes people can worry in ways that seem irrational to the rest of us. Olivia, Scott, and I weren't able to talk her out of it."

"That's sad." Although BB had thought little about Nancy, Scott's genes were part of her.

Izzy nodded.

"What else is in your bag?"

Izzy searched through the contents and pulled out the packages labeled S7 and B2. These turned out to be a bicycle bell and three tiny plastic bears. BB understood the bell for Susie but the bears for her seemed dangerous. A two-year-old girl might put them in her mouth and choke on them. Perhaps BB was beyond that stage and Olivia told Scott she'd be OK. That would be a good example of Scott getting to know her.

"You get the idea, don't you? They met every year to shop and think about whichever girl they weren't allowed to see."

"We get the idea." Susie pursed her lips. "Can we open them all at once?"

"I promised Olivia I would show you these, one year at a time but I'll go through them fast." Izzy looked for S8 and B3, then the next and the next after that. Before long they had a table full of toys.

Susie looked at BB. "What are we going to do with these?" She asked, scratching her temple. "I can't see throwing them out but we're too old to play with them."

"We're not too old to display them," BB replied.

"You're saying I take my toys and you take yours, then both of us put them on shelves in our homes."

BB narrowed her eyes and nodded. "That would work."

"There's one more thing in here," Izzy told them. "Look at this." She pulled out a statuette, a woman in a dance pose, leaning to her left, holding the hem of her frilly skirt with her right hand while her left arm was out with her palm pointed toward the floor. "It's Ginger Rogers," Izzy told the sisters. "Scott carved it in oak and Olivia painted it. It's the last gift from your birth parents to both of you." Izzy sat up tall and winked. "You'll have to share it." She paused again. "There's something I've been thinking about. Rather than splitting these precious gifts. Why don't we all move in together? I could buy a place by Lake Hopatcong, a house with waterfront but somewhere we could live year round. I have the money to get something nice. That way you girls can display all these on a single shelf and be together to enjoy them."

BB laughed. "Seems like a drastic move just to keep some toys together."

Susie reached over and gave BB a light tap on her arm. "Not just toys. Don't forget Ginger's shoes." She took BB's hand and looked into her eyes. "I missed spending my childhood with you. Maybe using this as an excuse to get together isn't such a crazy thought. We could give up our apartments. Have you ever been water skiing? I'd love to teach you."

BB felt breathless. Izzy was right. She and Susie had a lot of time left to make up for what they'd missed. She focused her intense, blue eyes on Susie's identical pair and said, "I'll try skiing if you'll go horseback riding with me. Or play tennis."

They hugged but Susie released BB when she heard a soft sound. She turned to see Taylor in the doorway between the porch and the living room. Taylor frowned, then lowered her eyes, and scurried off.

Susie excused herself, then followed Taylor. She found her at the far end of the room, around the bend by the dining room table. She was standing still but facing away. Susie went to her and put a hand on her shoulder, causing Taylor to turn.

"It would never work," Susie said. "I'm uncomfortable with being any way other than what I am. This differs from what you told Camilla because it's the real me. I'm sure of that. What's important is that everyone should be the person they are, right? Isn't that what *love is love* is about? Besides you're with Kyle." Susie hugged Taylor. "I need time to get to know my sister. I care about you but BB and I are what Mom's plan was about. We searched for the shoes and found each other. I think you should be happy about that."

Taylor leaned back so she could look into Susie's eyes. "Just kiss me," she whispered.

"Please don't push."

"You say you want to be fair, then kiss me—just once. I've stuck by you. I've been a friend. Do that much for me, all right?"

Susie nodded ever so little, and Taylor responded by pulling their faces closer and pressing their lips together.

At first, Susie felt as if she was going to choke but she tried to relax. *A kiss is just a kiss,* she told herself. She opened her lips. Her mind swirled and her heart beat faster. Kyle was in her head but it was Taylor in her arms. She had always loved the sensation of a French kiss. Now the slick feel of their tongues touching gave her an uncomfortable, tight feeling in her chest.

Taylor brought her hand down to Susie's ass and squeezed. This was too much. Susie stepped back. She had trouble catching her breath. "I can't do this. It's not right. I mean, not right for me, maybe for you, but not for me. I don't know why."

Taylor sighed. "You don't know what you're missing."

"I want to be your friend, Taylor, And Kyle's friend, too. I'm sure BB feels the same way. I hope we can do that."

Taylor smiled. "We can. You're right. I have two blue-eyed girlfriends and Kyle at night. I also have a feeling you'll never forget what just happened. Life isn't so bad." She shrugged, walked into the kitchen, and out of the house.

She's right, Susie thought as she watched her friend leave. *I'll never forget.*

* * *

Izzy purchased the house after the first snowfall, to get the best price. She put the title in BB's name. BB argued that receiving her inheritance while her mother was still alive was like something out of *King Lear*.

Izzy's eyes shone. "That's cute and I'm glad you know your Shakespeare but you're a dutiful daughter. I don't think I'll be ranting out on the heath."

Susie cleared her throat. "She won't drive you out but the weather might. I grew up in this area and the winters can be tough."

That winter was mild, but even so Izzy was stuck inside for most of the season. A problem she had expected bothered her. Few of her neighbors lived there year round and none of them, except Susie and BB, were theater people. Since Susie and BB both went to their jobs during the day, Izzy sat through many long, boring hours alone.

In the spring she put her name on the waiting list for residency at the Actors Fund Home in Englewood. Izzy had been contemplating this move for a long time which was why she had been so fixated on putting the lake house in BB's name.

Chapter Thirty-Two

When BB introduced Susie to horseback riding, Susie found the trail riding to be fun. But when they tried trotting in the coral, Susie ended up with a sore bottom that bothered her for more than a week. She swore she'd get revenge when she took BB water skiing but it would be months before the water would be warm enough for that.

The five friends were together constantly, even after Kyle and Taylor moved back to the apartment in Parsippany. Still, when Susie suggested they have a holiday get-together at BB's new house, Izzy insisted they treat it like a full-blown party. Susie, BB, and Izzy decorated the house with a Christmas tree, stockings over the fireplace, and lights out on the deck overlooking the lake.

BB was the one who suggested hanging mistletoe over the entrance to the kitchen. The frame was low there and that spot could be seen from anywhere in the kitchen or the living room.

Izzy had an electric keyboard so she and Susie switched off, each playing a mix of Christmas carols and songs from Broadway musicals. Everyone had a blast singing and drinking plenty of the spiked punch.

At one point BB got up and headed toward the kitchen to refill a plate of sausage rolls. Taylor followed and, when they reached the mistletoe, put her hand on BB's shoulder. Taylor asked, "Did you ever kiss a woman?"

Susie's head jerked back. It was the same question Taylor had asked *her*, the exact words. It had to be a line she used all the time.

BB's reaction differed from the way Susie had reacted. "Sure," she said, "and I wouldn't mind kissing another."

The kiss started stiff, like most public kisses, but soon Susie could feel the heat rise from across the room. BB even dropped the plate she'd been carrying. Fortunately, it was plastic and unbreakable.

They were both breathing hard when they separated. A moment passed, then they looked into each other's eyes and kissed again!

Susie felt dizzy as she watched. Her first thought was that she and her sister were as different as water and stone but her heart reminded her they were more alike than different. They were like Ginger's shoes, one left and one right but basically the same.

When the second kiss was over, BB said, "That was nice." She bent down to pick up the plate and continued into the kitchen. Taylor looked stunned. Susie had seen that look on a couple of men she'd known but hadn't expected a similar reaction from Taylor.

Susie thought of Kyle. She turned to look at him. He was the only one in the room more stunned than Taylor. She knew he had to be hurting. Even though he could be a flirt, it's always easier to picture yourself with someone else than to imagine your partner in that situation.

Taylor looked back at Kyle, then followed BB into the kitchen.

Susie moved to be beside Kyle. She put an arm around him and leaned her head on his shoulder. He took her hand and squeezed it. She could tell he needed her.

The rest of the Christmas party was awkward as were the next couple of weeks until Susie and Taylor talked and then changed places. Taylor moved in with BB and Susie went to live with Kyle. They didn't think anyone would object, and they were right. This meant Susie would live in Parsippany until the weather warmed. It was Taylor's apartment, but they were both fine with the arrangement. It took another couple of weeks after that move for Susie to move again, this time from the spare room to Kyle's room.

Chapter Thirty-Three

2023

In late May, an apartment in the Actors Fund Home became available and Izzy moved to Englewood. Kyle and Susie hosted a party to celebrate Izzy's move and the friendship they all enjoyed. They served a supper of grilled bass Kyle had caught, a salad Taylor had brought, and stuffed potatoes Susie had prepared. After they ate, they moved on to the main event of their big bash. Susie had set up the TV to stream *Top Hat*. Kyle, Susie, and Izzy had seen the film before but the other two hadn't. They all sat down with glasses of beer or wine and bowls of popcorn, then watched it all the way through without a break.

When it was over Susie asked, "What did you think?"

BB was the first to speak. "It certainly wasn't our shoes she was wearing in the park Gazebo. She had riding boots on. So I'm guessing it was the *Cheek to Cheek* dance. Her skirt was long so I couldn't always see her shoes but when I did I could tell they were sparkly and had high heels like ours."

Taylor put her hand on her heart and sighed. "Still, that gazebo scene was amazing. Can you believe how well that woman could dance in boots?"

BB reached over and squeezed Taylor's thigh. "You're right there."

"The *Cheek to Cheek* dance is also the scene Nancy was watching on Susie's eleventh birthday while she was holding one of those." Kyle nodded toward the table where he'd put Ginger's shoes. "So I agree with you."

BB pressed her lips together. "There's something else I noticed about the movie." She shook her head slowly. "The way it portrays love is a little silly."

"How so?" Taylor asked.

"People don't fall in love like that." BB blinked twice. "The Fred Astaire character takes one look at the Ginger Rogers character, dances with her in the park, and decides that's the girl for him. I prefer modern movies where it takes a little more time for people to figure things out."

"I fell for you right away," Taylor told her.

"That's different. You fell for me because I look like my sister."

Taylor's brows furrowed. "Ouch."

BB laughed. "Don't misunderstand me. I know you love me but it's taken time to get to this point and we've got further to go. Remember, you have a reputation."

"A reputation?"

"That you don't stay in relationships for the long haul."

"You can say *that* again," Kyle chipped in.

Susie stood. "Whoa. Calm down. Everybody liked the movie, right?"

The tension seemed to leave the room as they all agreed the film was great.

"I love those old musicals," Izzy said. "Sure they can be unrealistic but sometimes I need to see a show that's just fun."

They talked for another hour and were all in agreement that the film and the party were wonderful.

Since it was getting close to sunset, Taylor suggested she and BB head home. "We have to run Izzy out to Englewood and the less I drive in the dark the better. Besides, you need to take us off island and you probably want to do that before the no-wake rule kicks in."

When they reached Bridge Marina, everyone hugged and agreed the party was a fabulous celebration of a wonderful adventure. They all hoped they could share another experience like searching for the shoes.

When Susie and Kyle returned to the island house Kyle started to clean up but Susie stopped him. "Let's sit and talk," she said. "We can get this tomorrow."

"All right."

Susie sat on the couch and sighed. "They're good friends. It's funny how we can still get along so well after so many mistaken relationships."

Kyle nodded.

Susie patted the couch beside her, and Kyle took a seat. She leaned against him.

"I want you to know something." She was speaking in a low voice. "I loved you when we were kids. I didn't know how to put it into words. I was too young. But I loved you then and I love you now."

"I feel the same."

Susie held up her hand. "Wait. I have to say something. I agree with what BB said. Love in the real world isn't a simple thing like it is in the old movies. We don't just find each other and start dancing like Fred Astaire and Ginger Rogers. We have to grow into each other. Our history will help with that but I've got something special, something that will also help."

"What's that?"

"You'll see. I bought another film to watch tonight."

"Really?"

"Yes. It's *The Lion the Witch and the Wardrobe.*"

Kyle felt heat radiating up through his chest. "You are full of surprises, Susie Walsh."

"It's time for us to watch and reminisce."

"I can't think of a better way to spend the rest of the night."

Susie winked. "I can think of something and I'm hoping we can do it." She pulled his face toward hers, kissed him, then whispered, "After the show, let's go upstairs and cuddle in the wardrobe."

Author's Note

Many authors will tell you their characters write their stories. If the writers develop those individuals with emotional depth, the decisions they make are clear. Good writers allow their characters to create their own paths.

This process happens in all my writing, but in *Ginger's Shoes* it changed the direction of my story. Taylor led me along a path I did not originally think would be part of the story. She met Susie and felt the jealousy that would be normal when a person in a relationship meets someone their partner has talked about for years. But Taylor found she liked Susie and soon found she liked her in a way that was stronger than just a friendship. I had to go back and revise some of the earlier moments to reveal Taylor as a bisexual woman.

That choice led me to another decision, to have Nancy's early acting career include a role in *Last Summer at Bluefish Cove* (a play by Jane Chambers, which was important in the early years of the gay rights movement).

Suddenly, my story became much more interesting, especially when dealing with the perspective of straight women with lesbian friends. Another subplot in the story is the pain of women who have difficulty conceiving a child. I've done my best to understand that difficult situation and to portray both Lisa and Nancy honestly.

The places around northern New Jersey and specifically around Lake Hopatcong are all real. I consider Lake Hopatcong to be a character in this story, a soothing mediator who brings peace to the people who live on its shores.

I hope you have enjoyed *Ginger's Shoes.*

About Steve Lindahl

Ginger's Shoes is Steve Lindahl's eighth novel. His first three, *Motherless Soul, White Horse Regressions*, and *Hopatcong Vision Quest* are historical fiction stories wrapped in modern mysteries. In these books, the characters must look into their past life memories to find clues concerning crimes in the present.

His fourth and fifth books, *Under a Warped Cross* and *Living in a Star's Light*, are also historical novels, but without the regression twist. *Under a Warped Cross* is set in the tenth century, in Scandinavia, Ireland, and Britannia. *Living in a Star's Light* follows the life of Lotta Crabtree, a nineteenth-century actress who achieved great fame and wealth.

His sixth novel, *Chasing Margie*, is the story of Margie, a young girl from an extremely wealthy family who goes missing in the early twentieth century and Sarah, a twenty-first-century woman of very modest means, who discovers she is descended from the missing girl and from the girl's fortune.

In *Woodstock to St. Joseph's*, his seventh novel, Gregory Hedden and his adult daughter, Corinne, are climbing the steps of Saint Joseph's Oratory in Montreal, praying for a miracle cure for his terminal cancer. Corinne feels responsible for the tragic accident that took her mother's life. She also feels guilt over what is happening to her father and is determined not to lose him, too. While they pray, their lives flash by, from the 1969 Woodstock Festival, where Gregory falls in love, to daily life in a Hudson Valley commune, where he raises his daughter with a great deal of help from his friends

Steve's short fiction has appeared in *Space and Time, The Alaska Quarterly, The Wisconsin Review, Eclipse, Ellipsis,* and *Red Wheelbarrow.*

Steve served for five years as an associate editor on the staff of *The Crescent Review*, a literary magazine he co-founded and he is currently the Managing Editor of *Flying South,* a literary magazine sponsored by Winston-Salem Writers. He loves to read as much as he loves to write and has posted hundreds of reviews on Amazon, Goodreads, Librarything, and his blog.

Steve is married to Toni Lindahl, a pastel artist. They currently reside in North Carolina. They have two adult children, Nicole and Erik, and one grandchild, Ava.

Acknowledgments

My wife, Toni, who always helps me keep my language clear and my stories on track, spent a great deal of time with this book and deserves much credit for her contributions. I also want to thank my daughter, Nicole, and my son, Erik. They both read an early draft and provided thoughtful criticism.

In addition, I appreciate the attention the writers in my critique group gave this story. They are Joni Carter, Ray Morrison and Howard Pearre, all fine writers and editors. The people I've met through Winston-Salem Writers have also been an inspiration through their discussions and examples of their own work. This is also true of the many artists I've met through my wife and her association with The Pastel Society of North Carolina.

Other novels by Steve Lindahl:

Motherless Soul

White Horse Regressions

Hopatcong Vision Quest

Under a Warped Cross

Living in a Star's Light

Chasing Margie

Woodstock to St. Joseph's

Social Media Links:

Website: http://www.stevelindahl.com/

Blog: www.stevelindahl.blogspot.com

Facebook: https://www.facebook.com/steve.lindahl.3

Amazon author page:
https://www.amazon.com/Steve-Lindahl/e/B0031GLA5Y?ref=sr_
ntt_srch_lnk_1&qid=1563058097&sr=8-1

Goodreads author page:
https://www.goodreads.com/author/show/3117087.Steve_Lindahl